About the Author

Jenny Valentine's debut novel, *Finding Violet Park*, was the winner of the Guardian Children's Fiction Prize and was shortlisted for the Carnegie Medal and the Branford Boase Award. Jenny's books have also been shortlisted for the Costa Children's Book Award, the Red House Children's Book Award, the Waterstones Children's Book Prize and the Booktrust Teenage Book Prize, as well as three further Carnegie Medal nominations.

Also by Jenny Valentine

Finding Violet Park
"A wonderful debut for many reasons... the book
is astute... full of bitter-sweet observations. The
plot is so well controlled that you never anticipate
the clever ending." *Guardian*

Broken Soup
Rich in sympathetic, unconventional characters
and precise observation, the book has a lightness
of touch that belies its skill... it is most enjoyable:
a life-affirming, witty, romantic read." *Sunday Times*

The Ant Colony
"[Valentine] has a magical narrative voice that instantly
engages, and her tale... is riveting. [She] writes so
beautifully and so convincingly that you're instantly
swept into the mystery of these people's lives."
Amanda Craig, *The Times*

The Double Life of Cassiel Roadnight
"Trust and treachery blend into a suspenseful, satisfying
story about the choices that we make." *The Times*

jenny valentine

fire colour one

HarperCollins *Children's Books*

First published in Great Britain by HarperCollins *Children's Books* in 2015
HarperCollins *Children's Books* is a division of HarperCollins*Publishers* Ltd,
1 London Bridge Street, London, SE1 9GF

The HarperCollins website address is: www.harpercollins.co.uk

1

ISBN 978-0-00-751236-2

Typeset in Joanna MT Std by Palimpsest Book Production Ltd,
Falkirk, Stirlingshire

Printed and bound in England by Clays Ltd, St Ives plc

For my Dad.

'The Gods envy us. They envy us because we're mortal, because any moment may be our last. Everything is more beautiful because we're doomed. You will never be lovelier than you are now. We will never be here again.'

The Iliad

One

At my father's funeral, after everything, I lit a great big fire in his honour, built from stacked apple crates and broken furniture and pieces of a fallen-down tree. It towered over the scrubby piece of land I call the bonfire garden, and blazed, too far gone to fight, against the fading afternoon. On the lawn below me, my family gulped for air like landed fish. They clawed at their own faces like Edvard Munch's *Screamers*, like meth-heads. His mourners poured from the house, designer-clad and howling, lit up like spectres by the flames.

My stepfather, Lowell Baxter, ageing pin-up boy, one-time TV star and current no-hoper, stood swaying, dazed and hollow-eyed, a man woken up in the wrong place after a long sleep. Hannah, my mother, crumpled on to the wet grass like a just-born foal in all her credit-card finery, her gorgeous face collapsing in a slow puncture. She clutched at her own clothes, sobbing violently, but she didn't bother getting to her feet. I doubt she could remember how, she was so weighted down with debt.

I could have filmed them, preserved their agonies for repeat viewings, but I didn't. I did what my best and only friend Thurston always told me. I savoured the moment because the moment was more than enough. I stood back and watched them suffer, feeding fistfuls of paper to the flames.

I wondered if they'd ever speak to me again. I've always longed for Hannah and Lowell to stop talking.

They didn't behave that way when it was my father in the furnace. Neither of them was sorry to see him go. Before the fire, there was a service for him at the crematorium. Ernest Toby Jones, one of a queue of waiting dead. Lowell worked the room in a tight suit and Hannah wore big black sunglasses to hide her lack of tears, and shiny black high heels with red soles, same colour as her lipstick. High-impact accessories are my mother's answer to big occasions, in place of actual feelings.

I couldn't stand the thought of Ernest lying in that box with the lid closed, all dark and lonely and gone.

None of it made sense to me. I couldn't keep up. But like water putting out a lit match, the rest of the world closed over the fact of his absence, and ran on. His hearse moved through everyday traffic. Cars behind him on the road tested their patience on his slow and stately journey to the grave. Only one old man, walking with a stick, stopped as the coffin navigated a roundabout and met my eye, and bowed his head politely to the dead. Inside, Ernest's thin crowd spread itself out across the pews and tried to fill up the room. God knows who most of them were. They wore their dullest clothes and tuned their voices to the frequencies of sadness and loss. I sat on my own. I didn't want anything to do with them. The chapel's technicolour carpets looked like off-cuts from *The Shining*, from a shut-down Las Vegas casino. I wanted to meet the person responsible and find out if they were joking, or colour-blind, or just a fan of Stanley Kubrick films. I wanted to tell Thurston about them because he would get it and because on that day of all days I could have done with him there. And then I realised the carpets were chosen perfectly, because they took my mind off the elephant in the room, the rubbed-raw stump of what was missing, the lack of my father, the lack of Ernest, who was never ever coming back.

I didn't have him for long enough. That's the bare bones of it. I wasn't ready, once I'd found him, to let go.

"Do you want a song played?" I asked him, the week before. "When the curtains close, when your coffin goes through. Do you want a hymn or something?"

He thought about it for one waterlogged, morphine-soft moment.

"Harold Melvin and the Blue Notes," he said, and his voice sat like pea gravel in his mouth, sounded like mice scampering in a faraway attic. It took an age for the words to come out into the air. "*If you don't know me by now.*"

"*You will never, never, never know me,*" I sang, somewhere between laughter and tears.

Thurston threw a fake funeral once. He hired a hearse and his Uncle Mac drove it. I sat up front and even though the coffin behind me was empty, it brooded, like something moody and alive, and I kept thinking there was someone else in the car. Thurston walked ahead on the street at this slow, slow pace in a threadbare tailcoat and a tall black hat, a face like wet thunder, streaked with tears. It was a Sunday in the suburbs, Long Beach way, out by Rossmoor. People were washing their cars and tidying their yards and a gang of kids were riding their bikes in circles round a run-over cat. Uncle Mac just kept driving, slow as could be, following Thurston's lead with a great big smile plastered to his face. He didn't know what was going to happen next and he liked it that way.

"I trust the boy," he said, "'cause he's a genius."

I wasn't about to argue with that.

The kids stopped circling, people stopped mowing and raking and more still came right out of their houses, and everyone watched this funeral that wasn't theirs. You could see them wondering whose it was and what the hell it was doing on their street, on their weekend. And then when we had everyone's attention, Thurston reached into his jacket pocket at the exact same time I opened the car windows and cranked up the stereo, *It's Just Begun* by The Jimmy Castor Bunch. In one fluid movement, as the music gathered itself together, Thurston took four home-made pigment bombs and flung them out and down on the tarmac in front of him. He walked and we followed, stately and respectful, through a thick and billowing cloud of colour that swelled and rose and then drifted down, clinging to his tear-stained skin and his black clothes and to our sombre, bug-stuck car. As we emerged from the colour cloud and the song kicked in, Thurston started to dance. Not just foot tapping or finger clicking, not just any old thing. His whole body dipped and slipped and flowed like water through the music, the notes flinging him into the air and then low and wide across the ground until the smile on my face hurt just watching him, until I forgot to breathe. God, that boy could move.

Everybody but us was still, like we'd cast some kind of spell on them, like we'd stopped time but carried on travelling right through it. People stared. That's all they could do. It was the kind of funeral you'd long to have, the kind you'd see and then years later couldn't say if it was real or only a dream.

It was a moment, that's what it was. Thurston dreamed it up and handed it over to those Rossmoor people, for free. They had no idea what they were getting. They didn't know how lucky they were.

Ashes to ashes, dust to dust.

When Ernest's emptied body had hit temperatures close to 1000 degrees centigrade and been reduced to a shoebox full of strangely damp sand, cooling down for collection, I wished for a great burst of sound and colour, a celebration, a free dream. Instead everything was quiet and ordinary and shut down. There might have been a hymn, and people got up and shuffled out, looking only at the ground. We drove back in silence to his house for refreshments and small talk, for gin-laced cocktails and tiny, harpooned sandwiches on the lawn. It would have been so much better with Thurston there to help me. I remember thinking that. It would have been something breathtaking and spectacular.

I wasn't wrong.

In the end, it was my best and last fire. I went out into the garden alone. The heat had dropped out of the sun and the light was leaving. I took a deep breath. I lit a match, put it calmly to the petrol-soaked rags at the bonfire's skirts, and I waited.

And I wished with all my heart that Ernest could have been around to see it.

Two

Ernest must have given up on ever seeing me again when my mother called him at home out of the blue. We'd only been back in the country five days. It was a Monday morning and it was raining. The clock by his bed said 11.32. The nurse passed him the phone while it was still ringing. Ernest said if he'd drawn up a list of a thousand people it could possibly be, we wouldn't have made the bottom of it. We'd been gone more than twelve years. He'd quit thinking he'd find us a long time ago.

Hannah and Lowell had talked about it the night before. They'd talked of nothing else for days in fact, since before we left home, how she was going to play it, what she was going to say. Lowell told her to front it out and act like nothing had happened, and I guess that's what she did.

"We're back," she said to Ernest, just like that, like we'd been away for the weekend.

A wormhole could have opened on the other side of the room and Ernest would have been less surprised, less terrified. He looked around for confirmation that he was awake and alive, not dead already, not sucked back in time, not dreaming.

"Hannah?" He breathed her name into the receiver. "Is that you?"

I could hear his voice, small and tinny through the back of the phone, like a man trapped in a cookie jar. I stayed close and listened. I'd never heard my real father speak before, not that I could remember anyway. He'd washed his hands of us a long time ago, and that was that.

"Yes, Ernest," my mother said, assessing her face in the mirror, smoothing out the lines around her mouth with her free hand then letting go, facial time-travel, back and forth, back and forth. "It's me."

It must have stripped him right back to the bone, her sudden call, her carrying on like nothing had happened all those years. I didn't think about it then but I do now, all the time.

"God, this place is a dump," she said, over his stunned silence. "So grey and so cold."

"Is Iris with you?" Ernest asked her.

She didn't answer him directly. It's one of the few things about Hannah you can always count on – her lack of generosity, her guaranteed refusal to give a person what they want. The question bounced off her and she just moved right along.

"We've got some work with the BBC."

"News to me," I said under my breath, because as far as I knew, we'd been running from a mountain of debt and other trouble, not headed towards a bright new future. Hannah slapped me on the back of the arm and gestured at me to zip it or get out.

"It's a really good move for us," she said, "apart from the weather."

"Why have you called, Hannah?" I heard him say. "What do you want?"

My mother has a special voice for deal making. It's sharp and flinty, like a rock face, like gritted teeth. She locks everything into a safe and then she opens her mouth. "Shall we meet?"

There was a pause, just quiet on the line like he was thinking about it. The way I saw it, he wasn't exactly jumping at the chance.

"Why now?" he said.

"Don't you want to?" Hannah put her hand over the mouthpiece and hissed, "See?" like this was proof she'd always been right about him. I got ready to be rejected all over again. I hadn't been expecting anything different. It wasn't even that big a deal.

"It's not that," he said.

"So what is it?"

"I'd need you to come here."

I figured that was that. I was about to leave the room and get on with the rest of my Ernest-less life. Hannah told me once that Ernest lived alone in the middle of nowhere and that she'd never go back because it was just about the dullest place on earth, with no shops or Wi-Fi or bars or people or tarmac or houses. My mother was a fish out of water in a place like that, a bird of paradise in a cesspit.

"Just sheep," she'd said, "and grass. And Ernest," and she'd shuddered at the horror of it. "Never, ever again."

"Why's that?" she asked him now in an I'm-holding-all-the-cards, mountain-to-Mohammed, over-my-dead-body kind of way. "Why don't you come to London? I thought we could meet at the Royal Academy. You can buy me tea at Fortnum's, like you used to."

A trip like that was beyond him. Just getting out of bed was a half-hour operation, followed by a three-hour sleep. Ernest wasn't going anywhere. He said so.

"Bring Iris if you can," he said. "I'd really like to get another look at her before I'm gone."

"Another look?" I whispered. "What am I? A vase?"

"Gone?" she said, swatting me away. "Where are you going?"

"I'm sick," he told her.

"What's wrong with you?"

He paused. I could hear it. "Lung, liver, bone," he said. "Oh, and brain. I forgot to say brain."

He could have lied. He could have made something up, I suppose, but he gave it to her straight. He was dying.

I felt the base of my stomach drop out, just for a second, like it does on a rollercoaster, when you're at the top and about to tip over and it's too late to change your mind and go back. Thurston was always looking for that feeling. He said he went after it because he could never tell if it was the tail end of excitement or the beginning of remorse. I said maybe it was both and wasn't that possible and he said that was exactly why he liked me, precisely how come we were friends.

Hannah's pupils deepened like wells and she gripped the

receiver harder, until her knuckles went white. She made the right noises but they didn't match the look on her face.

"Oh God," she said. "How long have you got?"

"Hard to tell," I heard Ernest say. "Weeks, if I'm lucky."

"And how long have you known?"

"Not nearly long enough."

"And you're sure?"

"I'm sure, Hannah," he said. "It's over. I'm out."

I watched her wet her lips with the tip of her tongue, like she could taste something sweet. Hannah saw me watching and turned away. "She's sixteen, you know," she said, twirling at her hair with her fingers, sliding it past her teeth, checking for split ends. "Iris. Can you believe it?"

Ernest breathed for a bit, which sounded like someone walking on bubble-wrap, and then he said, "There are things I've been hoping to give her. Family things. It would mean a lot, to be able to tell her myself."

It didn't mean much to me one way or another, not back then. I was too busy working out how I was ever going to get home, worrying about how I was going to find Thurston. Family wasn't high on my list. Blood is no thicker than water, not when you've been on the other side of the Atlantic Ocean for most of your life, not when the one person you care about is still over there, and not talking to you, and you haven't had a chance to say sorry, or goodbye. Hannah looked at me, all worked up and wide-eyed, but I just shrugged.

"What things?" she said, too fast if you ask me, too hungry.

"Just some paintings."

"*Just some paintings,*" she echoed through her Cheshire Cat smile.

"If she wants them."

"Oh, Iris is into her art," she drooled. "She'll want them."

"So bring her," he said. "Come and visit."

She used this pouting, sugar-soaked voice to shake him down. "And what do I get if I do? Are you going to make it worth my while?"

I was ashamed of her, honestly. I didn't know where to look. And at the same time I thought maybe Ernest deserved to be played by her, that he'd made his own bed, after all. I definitely remember thinking about that.

"Let's talk about it when you get here," he said.

"If I get there," Hannah hardened up again, "not *when*. I can't promise, Ernest. It's not a given. I can't just drop everything."

I wondered what it was she reckoned she was carrying, what it was she'd have to drop, apart from credit cards and cigarettes and gum.

There was a silence then. I heard the loose wet rattle of him sighing into the phone. Hannah counted with her fingers, slowly, for my benefit, to show she knew already how this would go. She winked at me, like we were in it together.

"You'll be rewarded," Ernest said. "You know how generous I can be."

"I do," she said.

"Come soon," he told her. "I don't have much time left."

When she put the phone down she was glowing. She couldn't wait for Lowell to get back from his audition so she could tell him the good news. Everything about the way my mother moved around the room was different after that call, lighter, like she'd just mainlined a barrel full of hope.

I asked her how come Ernest was so keen to get eyes on me all of a sudden, after so many years of nothing. I didn't feel like humouring him. The last thing I wanted was to be the centrepiece of an old man's guilt trip.

"Who cares?" she said. "This is good news, Iris. Don't try and spoil it."

"Good news how?"

"Your father," she told me, "was a very wealthy man."

"*Is*," I said. "You just got off the phone with him. He's not dead yet."

"Yes, OK." She dialled Lowell's number, pulled a face. "*Is*. But he'll be dead soon."

I laughed. "You look human," I told her, "but inside you've got to be part android."

"Don't give me that," she said. "You know he left us with nothing."

"You've told me enough times."

"So don't waste your time sticking up for him. He's been a terrible father to you."

"And he's going to be a better one when he's dead? Is that the logic?"

Hannah hooked the phone between her jaw and her shoulder, and poured herself just an inch or two of vodka. Morning measures, Thurston called them. Breakfast of Champions.

"Get what you can out of Ernest Toby Jones," she said. "That's my advice to you, free of charge."

Nothing is free of charge in my mother's world. She never gave a thing away without making somebody somewhere pay for it. I knew her well enough to know we weren't in this together, not for a second.

"Is that what you plan to do?" I asked her. "Get what you can?"

"You'll feel the same way," she said, "once you see the pictures he's got on his walls."

"What pictures?"

"Priceless ones," she said.

"Which artists?"

She waved the question away with a flip of her hand and rubbed her fingers and thumbs together, the way people do when they can smell money.

"You've got me all wrong," I said. "I'm not interested in how much they're worth."

"You will be," she said.

"And how do you figure that?"

She smiled. "You think you're immune to the dollar," she said. "You think you're above all that, but you're not."

She knocked the vodka back with a quick snap of her head. I watched her swallow it, watched the mechanism working in her throat like rocks in a sack. Mother's little helper.

"To Ernest," she said, recalibrating her smile as the drink hit her bloodstream. "You and me and his millions are all he's got."

Three

Hannah and Lowell stayed up later than ever that night, getting reckless, lurching towards triple-strength cocktails and dancing in the living room. Neither of them had to be up for work in the morning. They probably thought they'd never have to work again. I could hear them talking about cruise ships and second homes in the South of France and film financing and cosmetic surgery. They were celebrating their sudden, soon-to-be fat fortune, counting their chickens, peaking too early, as usual.

I thought about the time Thurston and I talked about what we'd do with a vast, Forbes Top Ten Rich List, silly, unforgivable amount of money.

Change the world, Bill and Melinda Gates style.

Live on another planet, but only on weekends.

Get $10 bicycles for 4 million of the world's poor.

Buy United Technologies (or Fox or Walmart or all three) and close them down.

"Give it all away to strangers," he said, "face to face, in random, life-changing acts of generosity."

"Set fire to it," I said, "and enjoy the look on my mother's face."

He said that if by some miracle I ever got that kind of rich, I should be sure and let him know, and that he would help me decide.

"You'll be the first person I call," I said, even though I knew he didn't have a cell phone and never would. Tracking devices, Thurston called them, and he refused to be tracked.

A fine principle, I told him, an interesting stand. Worse than useless, it turns out, when you're trying to find somebody, when you want to tell them where in the world you've disappeared to, when you need to see if they're anything like even halfway to OK. After we left in such a hurry, I realised I didn't even know where Thurston lived. I never went there. He never told me. It just didn't come up.

I rolled on to my side and pressed a pillow over my head to shut Hannah and Lowell's noise out. I tried to think about Ernest. I'd only ever seen photos, one or two, of a serious, comb-haired, indoors sort of a guy, a bit of a geek, startled by the camera. They were yellowed and faded with age those photos, like they came from a different time, like they had nothing at all to do with me. I wanted to feel something about him dying, I knew I ought to, but really he was no more than biology to me. We had nothing in common, unless you'd count a total lack of interest in one another. His silence my whole life kind of spoke for itself. I grew up hearing it, as loud as any of Hannah's yelling ever got to be.

I'd taken a couple of pills from my mother's well-stocked bathroom cabinet and I lay there waiting for the day's sharp edges to blur into sleep. The sheets felt rough beneath me like thin cotton over sandpaper and my pyjamas twisted tight around my legs like a trap. I closed my eyes and imagined random objects in my bedroom bursting obligingly into flames, something Thurston taught me, a tailor-made way to relax. It wouldn't work for everyone, he said, but it sure as hell worked for me. Behind my eyelids, everything was torched and blasted with fire. My shoes smouldered, my alarm clock warped and melted, my bedding was ablaze. I felt like a superhero on a day off, like a plume of smoke, cloud-wrapped, buoyant. I couldn't move but inside I was flying. The skin on my palms seethed and bubbled. I was a burning candle, I was a pool of hot wax and then I was gone.

Some days inside my head there is nothing but fire. Most nights I sleep deep inside its bright, fast blooms. I have longed for it in random places – the old baths near our flat on Grafton Road, the vacant Embassy Hotel on South Grand, that copse of larch and ash beyond Ernest's garden, the painted house downtown where my mother went to therapy for a while and left me in the waiting room willing the fish to broil in their gravelly, weed-wrapped tank. My fingers itch constantly for the length and neck and strike of a match. My heart swells and soars at a column of smoke against the sky. I pine for the flame's lick, the sharp scorch in my lungs, the same way an addict pines for the needle. Thurston said once that I had the sweet moment of surrender all tangled up with love, and maybe he was right, but that didn't mean I knew the first thing about how to untangle it.

I tried to keep my fires small after we moved back here, small and secret. Hannah was watching me like a hawk, keen to ship me off to some correctional centre or other, now that she could do it on the good old National Health. I couldn't let her see me. I needed to be cleverer than that. A wastepaper basket, some old clothes, dry leaves, a length of rope, everything has its own flame. Everything burns at its own pace, with its own particular smoke and smell. I made fires every day because I had nothing better to do; little heaps of dry matter assembled and lit before breakfast, after lunch, behind buildings, on wastelands, on walkways and under bridges. I was fast and precise. I could start one in seconds, get up and walk away, my mind a little emptier, my breathing easier. Nothing got damaged, not by the small fires. They were actually pretty useful in their way, a kind of tidying up, an imposing of order and neatness on things. They didn't do any harm.

I was twelve, my first proper fire, and I was alone. I hid in a hollowed-out oak in a quiet dip in Griffith Park, dragging in gathered sticks and strips of bark like a worker ant. I was careful about building it. I took my time. I had a rolled-up old magazine of Hannah's in my back pocket for starting it, hungry looking ladies with tight trousers and tight smiles. I had to twist the pages just so – too loose and they'd flare out before the wood could catch, too much and they wouldn't burn at all. I'd watched Lowell do it often enough in the cramped, weed-choked yard of our apartment. Now it was my turn.

I only had one match. I don't remember where I found it. I held it up and even I could see how small and pitiful it looked, how unlikely it was to start anything worth bragging about. I breathed in and ran the match across the gritted bottom of my shoe, felt the stroke of it, heard the little pucker of air when it caught. And then I lifted it, burning, into view. It was thrilling to me. It was the start of everything, right there in my hand.

I shielded the tiny flame, moved it slowly so its own breeze didn't put it out, and then I touched it to the twisted paper. The smiling ladies writhed and blackened and the smoke rose in a rainbow of greys. When the fire leapt up I felt its heat, warped and dancing in front of me like liquid, like magic. I didn't know a flame could burn so many shades. I'm saying every colour in the world was in that fire, and watching it burn was the biggest, boldest feeling. I've never felt it again like the first time, not quite like that.

I got out of there when I had to, when the heat and the smoke made it hard to see and harder to breathe. I stayed low and made sure there was nobody around. My hands on the ground were covered with dust and ash. They looked like statues' hands. I moved away fast and then I stopped to watch the smoke from my fire rolling fat and dark as a storm cloud. At the top of the park, from the observatory, you can see way out over the endless fume-hung map of grid streets and thin trees and squat tower blocks and lit highways, as far as the horizon, further. My fire was a little insult to all that, something wild in plain view of the city. It felt like a door had swung open, like I'd been kept in an airless room all this time and finally I could breathe. I knew I should hurry, but it was like trying to run in a dream. Bright sparks and flakes of charred leaf floated down through the blue behind me, gentle as you like, and the flames licked and snapped like a dragon, biting clean through solid wood.

I couldn't see the smoke on the subway but all the time I knew it was there. I looked up and there was a boy, pale and dark-haired and skinny, older than me, fifteen it turned out, and he was holding up a handwritten sign and looking at me like he wanted to make sure I saw it. It read, WHAT HAVE YOU DONE? I went red hot and looked at my dust-covered shoes.

"Psst," he said, and I looked up again and a new sign read, WAS IT WORTH IT? DID IT FEEL GOOD? and I nodded and looked straight at him and we smiled.

That was Thurston. That's how we met. On the subway, eight stops from Griffith to home, he showed other people other signs and I watched him. He held up the signs and waited for them to notice, and the whole time he stayed looking at me. An old lady got WHERE DID YOU HIDE IT? IT WILL ALL WORK OUT FINE IN THE END. A shifty looking guy got LEAVE IT ALONE and YOU KNOW IT MAKES SENSE. A girl about the same age as Thurston, her hair tied up high on her head, earrings swinging, got BE A BETTER LIAR and OH. MY. GOD. Each time, they acted like he could see inside their heads and they coloured right up and couldn't look right at him again.

I loved it. I'm telling you, nobody had made me smile like that my whole goddamn life. I got off at my stop because I had to but I didn't want to leave and when I waved at the boy he winked at me and held up BOUND TO MEET AGAIN.

Back home, Hannah and Lowell were out, but they'd be back soon, crashing through the door and trampling on my quiet with their verdicts on the relentless heat, the price of everything, and the vital overall importance of their day. Much better, this peace, this alone time, this thinking about the boy on the subway, this picturing my fire. As it burned, I washed my hands and face, scrubbed the muck from under my nails, pulled off my clothes and hid them under the bed. The smell of it was still in my shirt, sweet and black and smoky. I put my face in the sleeve at the bend in my elbow, and I breathed.

I was hooked right then, on both of them, the boy and the fire. I don't mind owning up to that.

In London, I'd have dreamt about Thurston if I could. I'd have traded him for fire, but even in my sleep I couldn't find him. The next morning, the noise of the real world descended like a net and caught me in it. Somewhere a lorry was reversing, a car door slammed. I could hear Lowell making coffee, banging cupboard doors, and sweating out his hangover. I felt the weight of my own body like gravity, pinning me down in the wrong place, on this bed. I opened my eyes and everything was the same as the night before, unfamiliar, intact and unspoilt. No plain blue still-as-a-picture California sky but something lower and rolling and cold. No posters on the walls like in my old room, no piles of clothes or comic books, just unpacked boxes. No Thurston throwing stuff at my window, waiting on the corner so we could begin our day. No heaps of ash, no charred and twisted remains, just carpet and plaster and metal, and a father I'd never met and didn't want to meet, dark on the horizon like a storm. I couldn't have been more disappointed.

Four

My mother has four main stories she likes to tell: the edited highlights of her modelling career (who said what, who touched her where), her disastrous marriage to Ernest (no redeeming features), her many visits to Europe (ditto – Paris is littered with dog shit apparently, Venice is a rip-off and Florence is a bore) and the time she spilt a bowl of soup at the American Ambassador's house in Regent's Park. She never talks about anything real. She never gives herself away. It's like her life started at twenty-one, like nothing happened before that was worth mentioning.

"Maybe it didn't," Ernest said to me once. "Maybe things were awful," and it made sense, I suppose, of the way she drinks and thinks of everything as a fight, and grabs hold of the day like it's a sheer drop and if she doesn't dig her nails right in, she'll fall.

Back home, whenever we had people over, Hannah rolled out variations on her four stories while Lowell pretended to cook deli-bought meals from scratch, throwing his head back when he laughed, rattling pans and putting on a show. The moment the doorbell rang he was out on stage and she was prepping herself under the lights. I guess it made them both feel as if they were working. My job was to pour the drinks and play it like we were your dream family, like really the best of friends. We couldn't keep it up for long. Four minutes was about the limit. If we strayed into five, one or the other of us got bored or cranky and had to leave the room. There was no trace of our usual cook-your-own pizza and stay-out-of-sight arrangement. They didn't work their way through a bottle of vodka in old T-shirts if there were guests in the house. They hid the TV in a cupboard and acted like we spent our spare time holding hands and listening to recordings of T.S. Eliot reading 'The Waste Land'.

I used to think it was a miracle that anyone believed them. But people believe what they see. And mostly they see whatever is put in front of them, if it's in their interests to believe. Thurston told me that, and he was right. If someone gave you a fat stack of money and told you to spend it, you'd like to think the money was real. If they handed you a diamond and said it was worth as much as a house, you'd want it to be true, because you'd be getting something out of it.

The first and only time Thurston met Hannah and Lowell, he showed up dressed as a girl. More precisely, he showed up dressed as Hannah, wearing clothes he must have taken from her closet some time before, when I wasn't looking.

Lowell answered the door.

"Your friend's here," he said to me.

"What friend?"

"Charlotte."

I didn't look up. "I don't know anybody called Charlotte."

"Well she's here," he said, "and she's asking for you."

This girl came into the room, all long legs and lipstick and fingernails. Beautiful, flawless, just Hannah's type, the kind of girl I avoided like the plague, who wouldn't notice if she tripped over me in the street in her Manolo Blahniks.

"It's Charlie," she said, "remember?" Stretching out towards me, all grabby and polished, like some kind of sisterhood reunion. I looked down at her hands and I saw the little star tattoo at the base of the left thumb and it was only then that I knew it was Thurston.

"Oh God. *Charlie!*" I said. "So sorry."

Charlie was bespoke, made-to-measure perfect for Hannah and Lowell to fall in love with, an Orange County girl, drowning in labels, with money in her veins and parents who did, "Oh, I don't know, something in the movies." She dropped names in a way that made the sweat break out on Lowell's forehead, always the first name twice, to show how well she knew them.

"Leo, Leo DiCaprio's got one of those," she said, pointing to our crappy vintage-style blender. "Cate, Cate Blanchett would just love how you've done this wall."

"She's got style," Hannah said, watching her own skirt stretched tight over Thurston's narrow hips.

"Good manners," Lowell said, doing the thoughtful movie-star clench with his jaw, already wondering whether she had a crush on him, already working out how to get in with her people.

It didn't for a second occur to them that this was a piece of on-and-off homeless, skinny male white trash from the uglier side of town, graffiti maestro, street artist, performance poet and pickpocket, with a mild criminal record (trespass, jaywalking, vagrancy) and no sway whatsoever in the Hollywood Hills. Even if I had told them, right then I don't think they would have believed it. Just the week before, Thurston had strung a huge banner from the top of the Ocean Palms building, hand-stitched in letters more than two metres tall, FROM UP HERE WE ARE ALL NOBODIES. That wouldn't have meant a thing to Hannah and Lowell. There was nothing in that for them.

"Can I take your daughter out tonight?" Charlie asked, and they looked surprised as hell that someone so spectacular might know me, but they said yes, of course they said yes.

Thurston kissed them on both cheeks when we left and they didn't feel the stubble underneath his smooth skin, didn't notice the bitten-down nails behind the false ones.

"I can't believe you just did that," I said.

"No big deal," he said. "Everyone here is faking it."

"I suppose."

"How the hell," he asked me, taking my arm on the stairs, "does anyone walk in these shoes?"

We stopped at a restroom round the corner from our apartment. He'd stashed his clothes there, his baggy black T-shirt and ancient jeans. When he came out looking like

Thurston again, I thought he was a hundred times more beautiful than Charlie, but I kept my mouth shut. I didn't say so.

He grinned. "They loved me, right?"

"You were perfect," I told him. "How could they not?"

"Jeez," he said, "your parents are easy to please."

Charlotte didn't appear again. A while later, Hannah and Lowell asked me what happened to her.

I was reading about a sinkhole that had opened up out of nowhere underneath a man's house and swallowed his bed with him in it.

"I haven't seen her," I said.

"Why doesn't that surprise me?"

"I get it," I told her. "Too good for me, right?"

"Such great potential," Hannah said, like she'd know.

"I wanted to get her parents over at the weekend," Lowell said.

I suppose they wanted to believe I'd had a friend with connections, that it might almost make me somebody.

"She died," I told them, and I didn't care if they bought it or not. "She moved away."

Lowell's face hovered somewhere around shock at the

further thinning of his address book, and Hannah said, "Well, which is it?"

"Both," I said. "But not in that order."

They didn't bother to argue

Gullible works both ways. Tricking people requires their full co-operation.

"We're lazy," Thurston once told me. "We're happy to have the wool pulled over our eyes, because everything else is just plain hard work."

Five

I call my mother Hannah because she told me to. When I was about seven, she said it was time to stop being a baby and start using her proper name.

"Otherwise," she said, turning to enjoy her reflection from behind, "the older you get, the more you'll age me."

She is a beauty. You'd have to give her that. Tall and dark and glossy, like some kind of racehorse, with legs and curves that people feel the need to stare at in the street. We are not one bit alike.

I am plain-looking, skinny and flat-chested and small, and it suits me. I live in thrift-shop jeans and secondhand sweaters because they come in under budget and under the radar and they're just easy. I cut my hair short like a boy for the same reason. I've banked myself plenty of time and money by never minding too much what I look like. I think my day is about four hours longer than Hannah's without all the grooming in it. It's really quite liberating, not giving a shit. What am I missing out on exactly — make-up, brand anxiety and crippling self-doubt about shoes? Big deal. Poor me. If I was in charge, mirrors would be for making sure there's nothing stuck in your teeth or sticking out of your nose or tucked into your trousers, nothing more. I'm not likely to start staring into one and wishing I was different.

I used to wonder if that's why Thurston chose me, because I was unremarkable, because I'd be useful to him that way. Every hustler needs an invisible friend. He laughed at me when I asked him.

We were making him a mask out of old, broken sunglasses, sticking the smashed lenses on to a plain latex face, so that when people looked at him, all they would see was repetitions of themselves.

"I like you, Iris," he said, holding it up in front of his face, pulling the strap to the back of his head, "because you are you."

I was fourteen. I'd known him on and off for two years and he was the only thing I had worth knowing. It was the nicest thing he could have said to me.

My smile just about exploded, reflected at hundreds of angles by his mirrored mosaic of a face.

Hannah and Lowell think I am determined to be ugly. They think my attitude is aimed at them, out of spite. It's beyond them that somebody would go a whole day without looking in the mirror. They wouldn't dream of leaving the house without a layer of light-reflecting foundation and an accessory with a three-figure price tag. Looking good is the actual bedrock of their moral code. Presentation is ethics to them, which is why they bought me the dress. Hannah threw it down on my bed like a gauntlet, this loud patterned thing with a belt. I avoided it, walked around it like you would a patch of vomit in the street. I took a shower, pulled on yesterday's clothes and went downstairs for breakfast.

It was Saturday, the weekend after Hannah called Ernest and agreed to bring me (I think) for a price. Since then, you could see they'd been shopping. Lowell was pacing the kitchen in a stiff pale suit that made him look like a rectangle, like a man in a cardboard box. Hannah had on a mink silk top and a skirt so tight I wasn't sure she could move. I think she had to cross her legs the whole time to fit into it. They looked like they'd just stepped out of a shop window. I wondered how many hours the two of them had spent fantasising about the scene at Ernest's deathbed and the muted, elegant, expensive clothing they could suddenly afford to wear. I wanted to put a match to the hem of her skirt and set it alight, drop a hot coal down the neck of his jacket and watch it swallow up the fabric like a black hole.

"Morning," I said.

Hannah leaned against the kitchen counter, nursing a cigarette for breakfast. My mother often smokes instead of eating. She'd sell you a diet book about it if someone would let her. Her blown smoke bloomed in the bands of sunlit air that striped the kitchen, vanishing in its shadows, expanding to fill the room.

"Kiddo," Lowell said, like every morning, in his faked transatlantic drawl. "Nice of you to show up."

"Where's the dress?" Hannah asked, and I poured myself some cornflakes before I told her it was still in the wrapper.

"Aren't you going to wear it?"

"Nope. You should definitely take it back."

Hannah pointed at me with her smoking hand and an inch of ash fell soundlessly on to the soft suede toe of her brand-new shoe.

"Well you can't go like that."

"Why not?" I looked down at myself. "I'm always like this."

"Lowell," she said, still pointing. "Talk to her."

Lowell's jacket was too starched and too big, like the cardboard box was trying to swallow him whole.

"It's a great dress," he said, "really on-trend," as if his opinion mattered, like that would swing it. He talked like one of the girls at my old high school. I thought he'd fit right in there, simpering over labels in the hallways, bitching in the lunch queue about boys.

"So you wear it," I told him with my mouth full. "Help yourself."

"Just once," Hannah said through gritted teeth.

"Just once what?" I asked her, but I knew the answer. She wanted me to slot seamlessly into the picture-perfect lifestyle she had filling the space in her head, to stop being difficult and strange, to dress up and shut up and play along. We stared at each other. She looked away first. I always win that game.

Lowell had already given up and gone back to his magazine. There were lots of people in it he'd stood quite close to over the years. Things were happening. Men more successful than him were starting to lose their hair.

"Let her wear what she likes, Hannah," he said. "A dying man is going to have other things on his mind."

My mother put her hands together in prayer at the word 'dying' and looked up past the burst radiator stains on the ceiling.

"God knows," she said, "we could all do with a bit of good luck right now."

I asked her where she thought God filed that kind of prayer, the please-harm-others-for-my-benefit kind, and she ignored me. "In a box marked DAMNED probably," I said, "in a whole archive called *Be Careful What You Wish For.*"

"What do you care?" she asked me. "You're an atheist, aren't you? You don't believe in God."

"Humanist," I said. "There's a world of difference."

Hannah lit a new cigarette off the old one so she was holding two. She said, all deadpan, like it was the last thing in the world she was really thinking, "You must explain it to me sometime."

Thurston made a God box once. It was like a mailbox, with a slot, and he wrote on it PRAYERS ANSWERED. You were supposed to write your prayer and post it. That was the idea. He left it for four days on the corner of Westwood and La Conte, near the University. When he went back there was some trash in it, a couple of crushed cans, a banana peel and half a bagel. There was some angry stuff about blasphemers and the wrath of the Lord. And mostly there were wish lists, money troubles, exam results, job opportunities, and a couple of lonely hearts. My favourite one was written in pencil on a square of pink paper – THAT THIS BOX IS FOR REAL.

My cornflakes were stale and chewy. The milk was on the turn. New outfits aside, it hadn't been a good month money-wise, again. I knew that's why we were doing this. Hannah had slot-machine eyes, especially now she knew Ernest was on his way out. She was desperate to get there and clean up. Beneath the surface she trembled with it, like a greyhound on the starting blocks, like a size zero bull at a gate.

"When did you last see him?" I asked.

"When did he abandon us? I don't know. Thirteen years? Fourteen? Maybe twelve. When was it, Lowell?"

Lowell shrugged. "Beats me."

I pushed my bowl away. "And why are you all dressed up, exactly? What's with that?"

"We've got to look like we're doing well," she said, pinching a strand of tobacco from the surface of her tongue without smudging her lipstick, the same smashed cherry colour as her nails. "I don't want him thinking we need his money."

As if a new outfit could do that. As if a throw-up dress or a stomach-bug brown suit would hide our flock of overdrafts, a good silk blouse erase the sly and bottomless need from our eyes.

"Why do you care what he knows?" I said.

"We're going in there with our heads held high," said Lowell.

"And coming out with our hands full, right? To the victor the spoils?"

I didn't want a thing from Ernest. I didn't want to know him. I thought they should go without me. I had my eye on a clean conscience and the place to myself. I'd exercise control, build a fire in the grate and feed it kindling so it stayed small but never went out. I'd write letters to Thurston at all the addresses I could think of – the bar where Uncle Mac drank, the record store he liked in Echo Park, everyone at my old apartment building. I'd track him down so I could tell him what had happened, where on Planet Earth I was. I'd leave the lights off and the blinds down, be nothing but a glowing, empty house. I wasn't interested in helping Ernest feel better about himself. I didn't have room to play suck-up to my sick old stranger of a father for what he might be leaving me in his will.

"Do I have to come with you?" I said.

Hannah smashed out her dead cigarette on a plate like it had done something to offend her. She pulled on the other one so hard her cheeks caved in and I thought she'd smoke the whole thing down in one breath. She saw me, and I knew what she was thinking. Gone were the days when Little Miss Arson could be left alone in the house. There wasn't enough insurance money in the world that would pay for that.

"Yes, you have to come," she said. "It's *you* he's interested in."

"Oh yeah?" I said. "Since when?"

Her fingers drummed hard on the worktop and she declined, as usual, to answer the question. "It's not optional. We're not negotiating."

"I'm a cone in your parking space," I said. "That's it, isn't it? I'm a marker on your property."

"Think of it as a holiday," Lowell suggested, the shoulders of his suit rising up for no good reason to meet his ears, his right cuff already streaked with butter. "You can explore the garden. You can bring your bike."

I looked at him. "What am I? Eight?"

"God forbid we're there long enough for a bike ride," Hannah said.

Lowell stuck with it. "You can walk, or swim in the river. Maybe he's got a boat."

"An outward-bound holiday in a dying man's house?" I said. "Nice. Sensitive."

Hannah smiled coldly at me.

"Let's be honest," I told her. "You're going fishing and I'm the bait."

"It's remote," she said. "It's isolated. He's got acres of land, and woodland. It's a great place for a fire. You could light ten of the damn things out there and nobody would even notice. You're coming and you're going to like it."

I didn't look up. I kept my eyes on my cereal bowl. "Who else is going to be there?"

"Just us," Hannah said. "Ernest's been on his own for years."

"How do you know?" I said.

She bent towards her reflection in the side of the toaster. It was warped and squat and gauzy. "I just do," she said, baring her teeth to check for stains. "Trust me."

My chair legs scraped loudly against the floor as I got up. "Why the hell would I start doing that?"

I rinsed my bowl in the sink. Through the window, I could see next-door's cat lurking on the fence by the bird feeder, waiting to take one out mid-flight with a swipe of its paw.

It was the start of the summer. I had plans.

Hannah played with her lighter, grinding the flint back and forward with her thumb, holding the gas down, looking right at me over the flame.

"Is he at death's door?" I said, and (may God forgive me), "Will it be quick?"

"Cross fingers," she smiled, and Lowell got up to start packing the car.

Six

We drove towards Ernest on a bright clear day. He said he woke up to the dry powder blue of the sky and he knew we were coming. The Severn Bridge looked like the entrance to Heaven in an old film I'd seen about a pilot who'd rather not die yet, thanks all the same, because he's just met a nice lady and only recently started to enjoy himself. The service station on the other side where we stopped for coffee looked like the mouth of Hell.

Later, much later, I told Ernest this. We were playing cards. He said I played poker like a professional. Apparently, I shuffle like a croupier.

"And by the way," he told me, "it's only in a film you can decide not to die because your life has taken a sudden turn for the better."

I smiled, and kissed him on the forehead, and fanned

the whole deck of cards out with one snap of my hand.

It was Thurston who showed me how to handle cards. He knew hundreds of tricks. He had this one where the card you chose would end up ripped in half in your back pocket and he wouldn't ever tell me how it was done. "Magic" was all he said whenever I asked him. He said his Uncle Mac taught him but I knew that was a lie because I once saw Mac try to shuffle a deck and it was like he was doing it with his feet. By then I knew that Uncle Mac wasn't even his uncle, just some guy he'd met at a hostel, just another stray like me.

I thought about Thurston in the car all the way to Ernest's place. I remembered the look on people's faces when he pulled that card trick, the wonder, like he'd given them just what they'd been hoping for, like they were kids again just for a second, until they leant in towards him and said, "How?"

Partly, I was glad he'd never told me. It would have ruined it, probably, to know.

Four hours after we left home, we drove into Ernest's garden like tourists, suitcases piled up in the back, shopping bags and a black collapsible bicycle crowding at the windows to get out.

"If he's dead already, it all stays in the car," Hannah said.

I opened my window, which was tinted and stole the colour from everything, like driving in black and white. The house was a warm golden yellow in the sun, tall with dark latticed windows and narrow brick chimneystacks. Lowell turned the car on the gravel drive and it scuttled over the stones like a roach. To our left was a copper beech hedge, the colour of old coins, to our right a view of the vivid green garden through an iron gate in the wall. The wind moved in the leaves and I could hear birdsong, and music coming from somewhere inside. I tried to picture someone lying upstairs in a darkened room, listening to a violin concerto, reeking of decay and disinfectant while we swooped in to stake our claim. I wondered if he heard the growl of our tyres on his gravel, the beat of our wings.

"Look out, Ernest," I said. "Here come the vultures."

Lowell braked too hard and the bike caught me on the side of the head with a punch.

"Ouch!" I said.

Hannah retouched her make-up, pressed her lips together. "Be quiet, Iris. If you haven't got anything nice to say then don't say anything at all."

I wanted to ask if, under those rules, any of us might ever speak again, but I kept my mouth shut.

Ernest wasn't dead, not yet. He wasn't on his doorstep to meet us either. Lowell brought the car to a halt and frowned into his rear-view mirror. Birds scattered and resettled at the tops of trees and the front door stayed shut, as if nobody was in. Hannah balled her hands into fists and took an in-breath that didn't seem to end. Lowell passed her a paper bag and she breathed into it in quick little sips and flapped her spare hand back and forth in front of her face.

"Are you hyperventilating?" I asked. I'd never seen anyone do it in real life before.

She let out a high-pitched whine like a steam kettle.

"Stay calm," Lowell told her, reshaping his Superman kiss-curl with one finger. "We're on the home straight."

"Yeah," I said, "maybe he's kicking it right this minute. Cling to that hope."

Truth is, I felt pretty high-pitched myself. My head was full of white noise and I couldn't sort one sound from another, like everything was demanding to be heard at once, like I'd been turned inside out and exposed to the loud air. I don't suppose I expected to feel normal. It's not every day you get to meet the dad you never had.

Lowell and my mother clamped iron smiles to their faces and we got out, slamming the doors behind us. I turned my back on the house and looked out over the garden, across the fields, towards the woodland and the distant, shadowed hills. I breathed. Some species of tree are specially adapted to withstand and encourage fire. Some rely on it for their survival, to ensure their domination over other species, and to clear the soil and canopy for new growth. Trees look like their own shadows when they're burning. Flames fan out and eat up a hillside, way quicker than you'd think.

The front door swung open just as Hannah and Lowell reached it. The nurse must have run down as soon as she saw us.

"Welcome," she said. "Do come in."

Hannah and Lowell acted like they hadn't seen her. They know how to treat staff, how to exploit a potential VIP situation with disdain and to their own advantage. They learnt that, at least, in the States, if nothing else. I caught up and followed them in, met the nurse's eye, tried to say in a smile that I was sorry about them and that I wasn't the same. I wasn't sure if she got it.

The square entrance hall had deep tall windows and a high-backed chair drawn up to the fireplace. The walls were washed grey, and on the dull stone floor a thin bright yellow rug marked the pathway to the staircase, like the sun's pathway on the sea. I thought my shoes would leave marks on it, but they didn't.

Ernest might have had minutes to live but we still took our time about it. We had to check on the state of the art before we checked on him. First, Hannah wanted to show us the Joan Miró in the old kitchen, the Chagall lithographs and the Braque in the hall. She went all weak-kneed at the Picasso prints and the Modigliani in the dining room.

"I had that valued ten years ago," she said to Lowell behind her hand, whispering, "*over four million.*"

Lowell put his hand on her arm and gave it an imagine-what-it's-worth-now squeeze.

They were like this couple I saw at a gallery once. She was wearing silver jeans, I remember, and the sound of his boots on the gallery floor were like gunshots, shouting look-at-me, look-at-me, look-at-me. They wanted to buy a painting. They didn't even care which one. They just stood in front of the brightest and the loudest and said, "How much?"

I thought of them while Hannah and Lowell grinned up at the Modigliani.

"Tip of the iceberg," she said, beaming at him like she'd swallowed a torch.

However rotten their core, I have to admit Lowell and my mother make a handsome couple and a damn good entrance. I watched them getting into character on the way up the stairs, walking with their shoulders back and their stomachs sucked in, shutters down on their eyes and catwalk sneers on their faces. It was like Fashion Week had arrived. The mannequins, Thurston used to call them, the rare times they came up in conversation; mannequins one and two. As in, Thurston: Will mannequin one let you stay out that late? Me: She won't even know it. Thurston: What does mannequin two do all day? Me: Mirror work mainly.

"You never get a second chance to make a first impression," Lowell told me once, and I had to stop myself from pouring petrol over his shoes and lighting it up right there and then.

We let the nurse take us up but we could have found the room ourselves by following its sweet-sharp, metallic, medical stench to the first floor. It smelled pretty terrible in there. At the door, my mouth dried up and all the bones in my spine started singing. I'd have run away if I could, if it wasn't already too late. Ernest was propped on a few extra pillows in his sparse, stone-coloured bedroom, kind of sitting up when we came in. I felt white hot when I looked at him. I was half-drowning in pins and needles, top to bottom, but I didn't take my eyes off him, not once.

Lowell shook his hand too hard, pumping it like a man trying to get water from a dried-up well. This is his audition handshake, two-handed, the one that goes with unnerving amounts of eye contact and exposed teeth. Somebody somewhere must have told him it was a good one and he has tried, once or twice, to teach it to me. Ernest yelped a little when it started up and then he held on tight and brought the thing to a stop, like a galloping horse. Somewhere in his head I swear he was Gary Cooper, or John Wayne, just for as long as that handshake. I thought his shoulder might dislocate. I thought his arm might snap clean off.

"Hello, old chap," Lowell said, the country house vibe already seeping into his language. "Great to meet you."

He looked so healthy next to Ernest it was almost an insult. Lowell's teeth are toilet-bowl white. His eyebrows are plucked. He has shiny Ken-doll hair, not a strand out of place. He is tanned and well moisturised, still a catch. The carcass looks good, but I'm saying inside there is nothing but air. If you punctured Lowell Baxter with a pin he would shrivel to nothing, loud and aimless like a balloon.

Ernest didn't speak. I guess dying people don't much go in for small talk. It's not that they're more honest; I just don't think they have the time.

My mother stood behind Lowell, tapping her foot, and when he stepped back, she moved in, smiling too hard, like something sweet had stuck her teeth together. She bent to brush her cheek against Ernest's and her arms slid around his neck like snakes.

"Ernest, darling," she drawled, the words spooling from her mouth like cold syrup. "How are you feeling?"

She didn't need to ask. You could see how he was. There was nothing but sickness in that room, with its drawn curtains and watering eyes and thinning skin. Ernest looked about twice his age, like if you held him up to the light, you'd see straight through.

Hannah tried to ditch her gloating expression but it stuck to her face like the wind had changed. "I hope you're not in too much pain," she purred, stroking the front of his vest like a cat fixing to climb the curtains. Jesus, she was so damn obvious.

I stood in the doorway and let myself look back along

the hall so I didn't have to watch any more. Through a half-open door I saw a bright room with books piled on tables and curtains lifting in the breeze and a sofa in front of a cold fire. I'd have been happier in there – anywhere but here, probably, seeing all this. Next thing I knew, Hannah pulled me right into the room and pushed me towards him.

"Here's Iris," she said, like I was a clause in their contract, the parcel she'd been paid to deliver.

Ernest reached for my hand with his candle-wax fingers and I steeled myself and let him take it. His palm was damp and cold against my skin.

"Hello," I said, and my voice shook, my whole body hummed with the high-level strangeness of it all.

Later, Ernest said his larynx felt like a wood chipper. Great branches of thought passed through it and came out as nothing but dust. Here I was, and his damn voice wouldn't work. He smiled, he said, because that's all he could do, and there wasn't a word on earth good enough for him to use anyway.

I was all set to feel angry or sad or bewildered, and I think I was all of those things, and more. When Ernest smiled, the creases on his face stacked like towels in a showroom, like pieces of a puzzle. How many times do you have to smile to carve such deep lines in your cheeks? Ten thousand? One million? If a person spends twenty years of their life asleep, how many weeks of it do they spend smiling? How much does that vary, from the saddest to the happiest life? How could this man have turned his back on me? These are the things I was thinking the first time I saw his face. I think I smiled back though, and I didn't let go of his hand, not until I had to. Ernest was marooned on the white-pillowed island of his bed, with Hannah and Lowell swimming around him in ever-tightening circles like sharks, and he clung on to me like I was the one who could help him. I didn't know how to feel about that. I told myself this was my father, my actual flesh and blood dad, and I just about rode that wave but I had no idea what was supposed to happen next.

Spending time with Thurston, I'd got used to that lip of a cup, edge of a drop feeling, like it was a good thing. He was always pulling stunts, winding things up and seeing which way they went. Like when he stood at the Mall in Lakewood in a suit pinned thick, collar to ankle, with $10 bills (some of them real, most of them made with a scanner) shouting FREE MONEY over and over again like some garbage truck Wizard of Oz scarecrow. My job was to wait for the reaction, to watch and remember, no filming, no recording allowed, just as a witness. Other people filmed him. There were more than enough phones in the place for that. At first people flowed around where he stood, avoiding him like a rock in the river, and then somebody reached out. I remember the first hand, and then all of a sudden they were like bees to honey, like locusts, and I couldn't see Thurston at all until they'd stripped his suit bare and he was left there, spun and dazed and smiling, clean as a picked field. Afterwards he said it wasn't about the money, it was the moment, the story they got to tell. It was for the look on people's faces when they said, "You're kidding. That happened for real?"

Sometimes the most exciting part was the waiting. At Ernest's house that first day, I told myself I knew my way around the what-happens-now better than anyone else in that room. Thurston might not be here to help me but I could hear him anyway, telling me to breathe, and sit back, and not be afraid, and just let it come.

The nurse shifted in the corner.

"Who is that?" Hannah asked.

Ernest didn't stop looking at me.

"Lisa," he whispered in a voice like dry straw. "Or Dawn."

"It's Dawn, Mr Jones," she said.

"And who is Dawn, please?" Hannah showed her teeth in place of a smile.

"Dawn is the day," Ernest mumbled.

She smiled. "I'm one of the nurses. There are two of us looking after him. I do the dayshift and Lisa does the nights. Oh and Jane comes in to cook. She's been cooking for Mr Jones for—"

"How charming," Hannah interrupted, her face pinched, her voice stretched tight like a twisted rag. She sighed, already bored, and looked out of the high windows at the cloud-washed, Turner-painting view. Lowell hovered with his hands at his sides, clenching his lantern jaw, rocking on his feet in that suit, waiting for her next instruction. Ernest closed his eyes. Whole continents must have shifted. Glaciers formed. The land must have pressed together into mountains before he opened them again, and squeezed my hand, and said, "I'd know you anywhere. Isn't morphine the damndest thing?"

"We'll stay a couple of days," Hannah said, because she reckoned that's all Ernest had left. "Go and get your things from the car," she told me. "Take the yellow room. Lowell, we'll have the blue."

"Lowell?" said Ernest.

Hannah and Lowell stopped moving. They stopped dead for less than a second, like a break in transmission, but I noticed it still. The nurse cleared her throat and half put her hand up to speak.

"The blue room's Lisa's," she said. "I'm in the yellow."

My mother looked her up and down. "You're living here?"

"Yes," she said.

"Dawn is the day," I repeated. "And Lisa is the night."

"So we'll take the green room. And Iris will have to go in the attic."

"Whatever," I said. "I don't mind."

Lowell left quickly, ahead of her. I didn't move, not yet. Ernest was still holding on to my hand.

"Hannah," he said.

She stopped in the doorway and turned back towards him. She has great hair, my mother. It swings and bounces and falls, shining like dark lacquer, or an oil slick. She works hard at keeping it moving at all times. If she wrote a CV she'd have to add it to her list of skills.

"Yes?"

Everything Ernest was really thinking, he must have flattened and folded like a car in a crusher, and crammed into the quick look he gave her, like a library stored on the head of a pin. I must have blinked. Otherwise, I'm sure I'd have seen it. He'd have given himself away.

"Thank you," he said, a pearl of politeness after a lifetime of eating grit.

His mouth sounded as dried-out as sea sponge, his eyelids looked heavy as lead.

"Lowell," he said, looking straight through me.

"Do you want me to get him?" I said.

Ernest smiled and shook his head. "Lowell and Hannah and Iris."

I looked at the nurse.

"Don't worry," she said, "he's tired now. He'll brighten up later."

He closed his eyes and for a while he seemed to think he was in the garden, flapping at insects and muttering about the lavender. He held on still to my hand and the nurse kept busy in the corner, folding things, counting pills, making notes on a chart. The way Ernest must have seen it, Hannah came storming through the long grass towards him in her heels, and the long grass became the floorboards of his room and he was in bed again, not outside, and she was glaring at us.

"What are you still doing in here?" she said to me.

"Nothing." I let go of Ernest's hand. I pulled a piece

of thread from his dull green Camberwick bedspread and wound it tight round my finger until the end started turning from pink to purple. "Just leaving."

"So do it," Hannah said, her hands on her hips, a teapot with no spout.

"Is that a Vermeer?" I asked, pointing with my bound finger to a small painting in a deep gold frame of a girl in a red hat. The light on her face looked warm and real. Her mouth was open, like she was about to speak. "I love Vermeer."

"You do?" Ernest said, trying to sit up. "You know a bit about art?"

Hannah said, "She can bore you another time about that."

"It's lovely," I said, and she looked hard at me as if to say, "It's mine."

I unwound the thread from my finger and dropped it on the carpet.

While the nurse hooked up another bag of fluids to Ernest's drip, my mother bent to pull his sheets straight.

"If there's anything I can do for you," she said, more business-like than kind, "just let me know."

Ernest let his eyes roll back in his head. He started to cough, a wet thundercloud that rumbled through his body and left him weak and sweating on the bed. He hacked away until the noise drove Hannah out, and she drove me from the room.

"As if she had any bargaining power left," he told me later. "As if your mother had anything any more that I wanted."

Seven

Hannah and Lowell marked out their territory like tomcats, and Ernest's house soon stank of perfume and vodka and ashtray and under that something high like rotten meat. I think it was their livers. The two of them drank all day, which was nothing new. You could always hear where they were in a house by the clink of ice cubes in glasses. Hannah's high heels left flinty marks on the floorboards and four-inch spike holes in the garden. She measured out her day in tight sealed boxes: two minutes for snapping through a magazine, two for a cigarette, two for looking in on Ernest, or whispering with Lowell, or barking at the nurses, or at me. She was killing time, waiting for the grim reaper to arrive, looking at her watch like he was late and she was paying him by the hour. She bounced from wall to wall, over and over, like a fly mapping a room.

Lowell prowled the perimeters of things, noticing himself in every reflective surface. He passed the time picking up ornaments and looking underneath them, like a secret service agent checking for bugs. It struck me that the way he moved was precise and considered because the one person really properly watching him do anything was himself. Now and then he posed at a fireplace or a window and turned his face so that the light hit him just right – screen idol, male model, action man. I would never accuse my stepfather of being the sharpest tool in the box but he has a pretty good instinct for flattering lighting.

Ernest made a big effort to be out of bed. The nurses helped him downstairs and wheeled him out into the sheltered courtyard, tethered to his oxygen, the ends of his nose and fingers slowly turning greyish blue. He sat with us, pale and sweating, swaddled in blankets, and looked out over the bright lawn while we were eating lunch. Hannah took in his waxy, unshaven face and his laboured, bubbly breathing and dropped her fork into her salad in disgust, like she'd ever needed an excuse not to eat. She scowled behind her sunglasses and lit another cigarette.

She'd already been to see Jane in the kitchen and handed

over her list of sugar-free, low carb, low calorie, no gluten, no dairy, organic, Californian-style, fresh-only demands. Hannah will only smoke her way through the very best ingredients. Jane was overweight, with marbled arms and legs and sensible shoes and a chin that flowed straight into her neck. You could tell she was more suet than tofu. She scanned my mother's recipes with her shiny raisin eyes.

"You won't get almond milk here," she said.

"So get it delivered."

Hannah was about a metre taller than Jane in her heels. They didn't look like the same species.

"He only eats soup."

"Well his guests don't. And don't screw up, or I'll make sure he fires you."

At the lunch table, Ernest's chin slumped low against his chest. The breeze whipped his hair about in little tufts like cotton candy. Jane and the nurses watched us from the kitchen window.

Hannah looked at Lowell, "I don't trust any of those women. Gold-diggers, I'm telling you."

"Well you would know," I said, and she glared at me, and flicked ash into her lamb's lettuce.

"This is different."

"In what way?"

Hannah looked over at Ernest. "We're family."

I laughed. "Family? Since when?"

"Since I said so, Iris," she said, standing up before the rest of us had finished. "Since we came here to get what we deserve."

She went inside to get herself another drink. Lowell left the table too. That day he was on a pretty short leash. Ernest opened his eyes and winked at me. At least I think he did.

"I thought you were asleep," I said.

He shook his head. "Resting. Listening."

"I'm sorry for what you heard."

He pulled the blankets tighter around him even though the sun was out, and pretty warm. "No need. I'm sure she's said worse."

"It's pretty much your own fault," I said.

"What is?"

"I don't know. All of it."

He closed his eyes again. "I see."

"Have you ever seen *The Royal Tenenbaums*?" I asked him.

"Is it a painting?"

"No, a film."

"About what?"

"About a group of grown-up child prodigies who get together because their dad is dying."

"And you like it?" he asked me.

I nodded. "*Family isn't a word. It's a sentence.*"

I looked out across the fields towards the black shadows of the mountains.

"It's good to see you, Iris."

"You should have invited me sooner," I said, and it sounded more spiteful than I meant.

Ernest looked at me but I didn't take my eyes off the view. "You and I need to find more reasons to be alone together," he said.

"We do? Why?"

"We have a lot to talk about."

"Like what?"

"There are some things I'd like you to know," he said. "Things about me. About you and me."

There were tubes running into the back of his hand, stuck down with tape. His veins looked risen and solid, like twigs.

"Not to be rude or anything," I told him, and we both knew I meant the exact opposite, "but isn't all this a bit late?"

"I couldn't have put it better myself," he said.

"So what's the point then?" I said. "Are we just making nice?"

Ernest sighed. He sagged slowly, the way an inflatable does when the party's over and the air's leaking out.

"We can fight if you like," he said. "We can do all of that. It's your choice. But I want you to know, we might not have time to make up."

Jane came outside to clear the plates. Her cheeks were the colour of raspberries. The bony points of her body, her knuckles and elbows and wrists, were lost in her flesh, like someone inside a duvet.

"How are you, Mr Jones?"

"Still alive," he said drily. "Always a bonus."

We could hear Hannah inside the house, raising her voice over something.

"Are my guests being difficult?"

She looked straight at him. "I don't know who she thinks she is."

"The lady of the house," Ernest told her. "My wife."

"You're still married?" I said. "You're kidding."

Ernest nodded. "Twenty-one years this November."

Jane's jowls shook like a Basset Hound's. "Is there anything else I can get for you?"

"A bottle of the widow," he said, "and four glasses."

"Should you be drinking, sir?"

"No."

"Is it wise?"

"No," he said. "But I don't think it'll be the thing that kills me, do you?"

Jane frowned.

"We're celebrating," he said. "I'll just taste it." He put a hand on her arm. "And thank you, Jane, for asking."

She carried the loaded tray back across the grass, her apron caught in her waistband, her thighs like bolster cushions in her jeans. It was nice, the way she spoke to him, like it was her job, but she cared about him anyway. I liked her for that, even if I didn't like Ernest all that much.

"What are we celebrating?" I said. "Your long and happy marriage?"

Here I was, thousands of miles away from home, worried about Thurston, trapped in the wrong place, a pawn in some old war between Ernest and my mother. Honestly? It wasn't a champagne moment for me.

He leant back in his chair, blinked up at the sky and tried his hardest to breathe.

"I'm not sure yet," he said. "We'll have to wait and see."

Hannah and Lowell followed Jane back out of the

house, trailing the bottle like iron filings behind a magnet. My mother was at the isn't-everything-great stage of drunk. She arranged herself in her chair and sighed loudly.

"Champagne," she said. "How marvellous."

Ernest looked at Lowell and pointed at the tray. "Do the honours, would you."

Lowell popped the cork and Hannah showed more teeth. I could see her eyeing the bottle, trying to calculate how much was left.

"A toast," Ernest said, raising his glass. "To us."

My mother's laugh was quick and shrill and high. "I'll drink to that," she said, as if there were things in the known world she wouldn't drink to.

"Hear hear," said Lowell.

"To family," Ernest said, looking only at me. "Whatever that might mean."

Eight

Thurston and Uncle Mac used to buy lapsed storage units and sift through things once precious enough to keep safe and now abandoned. He said it was like buying into whole lives. You pieced together what you knew about somebody from the things they'd done their best to save. Vivien Maier's photographs were found that way, her life's work bought in job lots at auction after she died. Thurston spread everything he bought out like a map and then photographed it, and each photo had the name of the person who'd owned it. Leonard D Theil. Marsha Louise Hunter. Margot Florian Jones.

Apparently, I reminded Ernest of his sister Margot. Sometimes, when the pain got really bad and he went to town on the morphine, he thought I was Margot, come to visit. He talked to her instead of talking to me and I pieced her together like one of Thurston's photos from the things Ernest said. I didn't set him straight. If he wanted to see his sister then let him. There was no harm in it, after all. In some ways it took the pressure off having to be me. I could just sit back and listen.

When Ernest said, "How are you, Margot?" I said I was fine. If he said, "Do you remember the time when?" I said, "No, tell me again."

He talked about this grassy bank at the foot of the garden. When he was a boy the gardener told him it was a burial mound for an elephant. The circus had come here in 1832 and the elephant caught flu and died.

"You can't do much with a dead elephant," the gardener had said, "except bury it."

Ernest wanted to dig down and find the elephant's skeleton the way an archaeologist unearths a dinosaur. He wanted to dust at its bones with toothpicks and paintbrushes but he wasn't allowed. The gardener said they weren't to disturb the dead and Margot said, "Quite right. Leave them where they bloody well are. They've had their turn."

"You said the elephant would come and haunt me as punishment for wanting to open up its grave," Ernest told me. "You warned me to listen for its footsteps at midnight and then you paced the corridor outside my room banging that drum until I wet myself in terror and you skidded off to bed."

I smiled. "Sorry," I said.

Ernest waved his hands at me. "Don't be. You were always worth more than the trouble you caused."

Ernest reminded me of an elephant. The skin around his eyes was thick and dark and wrinkled, like an elephant's eye. And there were so many things he couldn't forget.

"Do you remember that hollowed-out elephant's leg in the hall for storing umbrellas?" he asked, and I pretended I was Margot again and said yes.

"Where did it come from?" he said.

"A dead elephant?" I suggested, and Ernest smiled and said, "Oh, Margot, I've missed you. It's been far too long."

Once he got started I think he carried on talking even when he was the only one left in the room, like a juggernaut too big and slow to turn around in a hurry. He was telling his life from start to finish, and it didn't seem to matter if anyone could hear him or not. Sometimes I listened from out in the hall because I didn't want to go in and disturb him. I didn't want to interrupt his flow.

Margot got sent away to school but Ernest stayed home because of a weak chest and allergies and something else his mum called an indoor disposition and his dad called a damn shame. He had tutors for maths and science. His dad taught him French and some military history and his mum taught him everything she knew about her favourite artists, Caravaggio and Vermeer, Botticelli and Gauguin, Da Vinci and Millais. The family owned a handful of valuable paintings. If he promised not to touch, Ernest was allowed to stand on a chair with his face inches from the canvas and study the precise brushstrokes of Gericault's *Portrait of a Kleptomaniac* or the urgent, frantic sweeps of Van Gogh's *A Wind-Beaten Tree*. In the library overlooking the garden she gave him books too heavy to carry, full of paintings and sketches. She showed him tricks the early masters used with mirrors and crystals and candles to trap an image right there on the page. Ernest loved copying the way they caught a hand or a foot or an eye. He imagined the real person in front of him, a servant maybe, a relative or friend. He wondered what likeness he got, if any, so many hundreds of years later, in his version of a version of them.

I listened to Ernest's ramblings and I thought this was where Thurston should be, listening with me, sitting with his knees up and his back against the wall. He'd have loved it. They would have been instant, proper friends. I have no doubt about that.

Ernest said his parents thought it was Margot who should be sitting quietly and drawing, but when she was at home Margot liked to ride and climb and swim and row and shoot.

"Can you still serve a ball straight on to a coin eight times out of ten?" he asked me, when he was asking her. "Can you still scale a tree like a primate?"

He said she was proud of her mud-streaked shins and filthy clothes and uncombed hair. It was Margot who caught a fish with her bare hands and bashed its brains out on the stones of the shrunken riverbed. Ernest could only watch. She brought it home, gutted it with her penknife and cooked it over an open fire. Her parents said it was no way for a young woman to behave.

"Thank God," said Margot, pulling fish bones out of her teeth, wiping her mouth on her sleeve. "I have no intention of ever behaving like one."

She called Ernest a mummy's boy, and Ernest was so struck by the idea that he cried and proved her right. But he liked to think he protected Margot, in his way, from the sharpened arrows of their expectations, the bullets of their many disappointments. By being their constant companion, the child they could control, he took their attention away from his tomboy sister.

"Stand up straight," they snapped at him when Margot slouched past.

"Your hair is a disgrace," they said, looking the other way as Margot pulled herself backwards through the box hedge and cut across the square, flat lawn, her own hair stuck with twigs and dressed with feathers.

Ernest half-smiled at me in the hazy, shut-curtained gloom of his room. "I was always in trouble because of you, Margot," he said.

"One spike or two?" she'd say, and if he asked why, she'd tell him, "Because you're such a bloody martyr. Live a little, for God's sake. Stop minding so much what people think."

Thurston would have liked Margot too, by the sounds of it. He'd have approved of the way she was different to the rest of her family. He always said the best people stick out like sore thumbs, that the black sheep are the ones to watch.

"Look at you," he said. "You're nothing like who you should be."

"And you?" I asked him. "What are your family like?"

"Gun-toting, stranger-bashing, rage-twisted, tight-fisted creationists," he said. "I haven't spoken to them in years. I had myself emancipated in a court of law. I can't see how we're even related."

Neither of us spoke for a minute and then Thurston said, "Please don't ask me about them again."

Ernest told me that at eighteen, Margot eloped with a taxi driver and lost a small fortune at a casino in the South of France. A month later she ran off to New York with a camera salesman. She didn't bother to marry him, which made things simpler. Her parents washed their hands of her after her third affair, with an ex-airline pilot, and a bit of light smuggling. They paid off the judge and then they cut Margot off without a penny, which was what she'd wanted all along. She used to tell Ernest that being born into money had made them all worthless and unmotivated.

"Look at you," she said, teasing. "They may as well have pulled out your spine."

Ernest said she went to London, trained as a nurse, and joined a team of doctors working in conflict zones and refugee camps, in the paths of epidemics and earthquakes and hurricanes. She never once visited home.

She was done with it. She sent Ernest postcards from all the far-flung, war-torn, disease-ridden, beautiful places she wound up.

"*So very different,*" she would write, "*from the home life of our own dear Queen.*"

If his parents got to them first, her cards ended up in pieces in the bin and Ernest had to put them together like a puzzle. He marked each place in his atlas with a cross, so he could see at a glance where his sister was, and how far from them she had gone.

"Don't hang about, little brother," she told him. "Get out while you can. Times are changing. There's a whole world out there. Honestly, I do things that would turn your hair grey overnight and nobody bats an eyelid."

But all Ernest wanted to look at and think about was art.

"What good is the real," he asked me once, "when there are so many better versions of it to distract you?"

He stayed behind with his books and his paintings and his parents. When his dad died of a heart attack at sixty Ernest took over the family collection. He sent works to galleries and institutions on loan. He bought when the price was low and sold at a profit. He had a feel for it. He and his mum sat for hours at the feet of Rossettis and O'Keeffes, of Pollocks and Rembrandts and

Gentileschis, of Kahlos and Hockneys and Rothkos. She broke their silences with updates on the absent. "Margot would hate this," or, "I want you to sell the little Gauguin," or, "Your father would have closed this deal by now."

He disappeared and it suited him.

"You were right, Margot," he told me. "There was a whole world out there and I avoided it like the plague."

"You did what you wanted," I said. "That's OK, isn't it?"

He smiled. "But just think of all the life I missed while I was living my own."

I don't think Ernest believed his family were together in some form or another in the afterlife, waiting for him. He didn't expect to see them again any time soon.

Margot died in a house fire in Nairobi when she was twenty-nine. She would have been almost sixty by now. Their mum died on a flight from Colombia to New York. The plane ran out of fuel and crashed into a hillside on Long Island's North shore. That night at home there was a storm. Ernest had no electricity for three days because the winds had wrecked the power lines. Otherwise, he might have known sooner. He thought the trees were going to come crashing through his bedroom window. He was awake all night, waiting for it to happen. He didn't know yet that he was the only one left.

"I miss Margot," he said, when he remembered I was Iris and she was gone. "She was my best friend."

"I've lost one of those," I told him.

"It hurts, doesn't it," he said.

"It does," I said. "Yes."

"Her name?"

"Who?"

"Your friend."

"Oh, his name. He's a he. Thurston. Thurston Shaw."

"Marvellous name."

"Marvellous person."

"Tell me about this Thurston," he said. "What does he do? Why do you like him?"

"He's an artist, I suppose. Not just nine to five, not for money or anything. He just sort of lives it."

"Sounds reckless."

"He's brave," I said. "And smart, and colourful, and funny."

Ernest smiled. "And how did you lose him?"

I told him I hadn't seen Thurston since a week before

we left the States. I said he had no idea where I was, and I had no way of finding him either.

"We fell out," I said. "I don't think he was talking to me."

He smiled. "What did you do?"

I felt like crying. That doesn't happen often, to me. "I hurt his feelings," I told him. "I said some things I shouldn't. And then I got dragged here, so I lost him. He's a needle in a haystack."

Ernest nodded. "The world is a very big place when you're looking for someone."

"I miss him," I said. "And I don't know what I'm supposed to do next."

"Get on with the business of living," Ernest told me. "You don't have any other choice."

Nine

The second time I met Thurston I was burning leaves in an empty swimming pool on an abandoned lot over by Long Beach, repossession central. The pool liner was this bright grimy turquoise and the leaves that had fallen into it were copper and chestnut and desert red. I was happy. I remember that. I looked up through the thick, sweet smoke and he was standing on the edge, looking down at me. I recognised him straightaway, the boy from the subway, still tall, still pale, still skinny. Suddenly there was a point to things, a reason for them. That's what it felt like, seeing him again.

"Hey," he said. "It's you," and he smiled and jumped in, one hand on the side, landing light on his feet in the dry deep end.

The leaves spat and settled and he put his hand out across the fire to shake mine.

"Thurston," he said.

"Iris."

"Do you remember me?" he said. "From the subway?"

I nodded. "The boy with the messages."

"Did you start the fire on Willow and Melrose," he said, "in the bakery?"

"No," I said.

He dropped his head to one side, crinkled up his eyes. "Are you sure?"

"I don't do buildings," I said. "Not working ones. Not like that."

"But swimming pools are OK."

I shrugged. "I'm just tidying up."

He looked around at the weed-choked yard, at the broken lawn chairs and left-behind toys and smashed-up deck. "That's one way of putting it."

He asked me how old I was.

"Nearly fourteen," I said. "You?"

He smiled. "Nearly seventeen."

He picked up an armful of leaves and dumped them on the heap, but before he did it he asked me if it was OK. "May I?" he said. I liked that.

I watched the flames and Thurston watched me for a quiet, crackling minute.

"Sure. Go ahead."

Leaves have this tang when they're burning, like nuked fruit juice. I can't think of a better way to put it than that.

"You need a mark," he said.

"What?"

"A sign or something."

"Why?"

"Say which fires are yours. Show where you've been. So I know."

"So you know? Why do you want to know?"

He shrugged. "I wouldn't want to leave it so long next time, to see you."

He got these paint cans out of his jacket and started spraying the wall of the pool. His back was half to me and I couldn't see what he was doing, but it was over pretty quick and when he stepped back there was an eye: sharp black pupil, clean white ball, swirling bright circle of colour.

"Iris," he said. "That's you," and then he jumped up out of the pool like there was still water in it to lift him. I didn't want him to go.

"Use it if you want," he said. "See you around."

Back home I practised drawing it the way he did, until I got it right. Then after that I started leaving little eyes in all sorts of places; along my ride to school, outside our apartment, on the boarded-up windows of the emptied houses, their lightless rooms dark against the sky like missing teeth. It got to be a habit. It got so I couldn't stop. When I saw that eye up against a door or a fly-poster or a stretch of ground, I knew I was somewhere and that Thurston was somewhere too, noticing me.

Nobody really noticed me at Ernest's. It wasn't about me and that was fine. There was this tug-of-war going on – the nurses on one side doing what they could to keep him comfortable and alive, Hannah and Lowell on the other side willing him to die, giving it all they'd got. I guess I slipped through a gap somewhere in the middle, because it was the quietest place to be. I kept thinking that if I could just tune in to the right frequency, I'd hear the sound of all that struggle, the way a dog hears things streets away that don't even register with the human ear.

And then after two or three days of doing his best to hope for the worst, Lowell decided it was time to go back to London, or my mother decided for him, it's always hard to tell. He was happy enough to do it. He was up for a role in a daytime soap so he needed to get back and get to grips with his Yorkshire accent. I had no idea he was leaving until I saw him with his suitcase in the hall. He didn't even stop walking, that's how little I counted. He waved at me over his shoulder. He couldn't get out of there fast enough.

"You're going?" I said.

"I've got a job. An audition. They asked for me."

I followed him out to the car. "Since when?"

Lowell slung his case on to the back seat and slammed the door. He was somewhere else already. In his head, he'd finished filming, been taken out for lunch and offered a spin-off series of his own. I know that's how his mind works. The only thing that's ever mattered to Lowell is his big break, and he's kind of heroic, I suppose, for always charging after it, for believing without fail that it's just round the bend. He could take or leave most of the real world but he'd go to the ends of the earth for a sniff of fame. I guess that's how we ended up in LA in the first place, chasing Lowell's disappearing dream. It's an addiction of sorts, like Hannah's credit card problem, or my thing about fire. You'd have thought we'd all understand each other better by now.

"I'd say you're here to the bitter end, Kiddo," he said, and he winked because he really couldn't have cared less, and got in the car. My mother came outside and stood behind me as he gunned it up the drive and on to the road.

"Right," she said, clapping her hands together, turning back towards the house. "Let's get to work."

"What are we doing?" I asked her.

"Do you remember that place we rented in San Diego?" she said.

"Yep."

"Do you remember how the landlord had a list of every single damn thing in that apartment so that when somebody broke the lightshade and the sun loungers he kept all the money from our deposit?"

Hannah and Lowell threw one hell of a party in that place when he got a speaking part in a movie (third cop – he ended up on the cutting-room floor). The lightshade broke because four half-dressed people were swinging on it. The sun loungers got thrown into the pool. I was eight or nine. Three different men came into my room that night and tried to pee in the corner.

"I remember," I said.

"Well, we're going to make a list like that," Hannah said.

"Of what?"

"Of everything in this house. So we know what's coming to us when he dies."

"You're serious?"

"Room by room," she said. "If anything goes missing, I want to be able to tell."

"Does Ernest know?" I asked.

Hannah looked at me like I hadn't been listening. "Of course he doesn't know. And there's no need to tell him. He's unconscious most of the time. He doesn't even know what day it is."

"I think he does."

I'd started to think that Ernest was overdoing it a bit when Hannah was around. Not faking it exactly, but he got drowsier when she walked into the room. He sagged and drooled and aged. He was hiding from her behind the thing she was so busy seeing, which was how little time he had left.

"He's on his way out," she said. "He's half gone already."

"Nice," I told her. "Really soft-hearted."

"This is insurance," she said. "I'm thinking ahead. I'm protecting our assets. I'm trying to do the right thing."

Just to be clear, my mother has never tried to do the right thing. She wouldn't know it if it hit her square in the face. But she's a survivor, I guess. She knows how to keep her head above water, if nothing else.

She handed me a notebook and a pen.

"Start in the dining room," she said. "I know for a fact there's Baccarat crystal in there, and box-loads of eighteenth-century silver. Just count it and write it down. That's a new car at least, in one sideboard. You've no idea how wealthy Ernest is. And we haven't even started on the art."

"You're enjoying yourself, aren't you," I said.

"Don't take this the wrong way," she said with a straight face, like there was any other way to take it, "but it's the answer to all our problems. This is a fresh start for us. Ernest couldn't be doing this at a better time."

I walked away from her.

"Oh, and Iris," she said, her chin stuck out in fight mode, her teeth pressed so tight together I could see the line of her jaw. Hannah has this thing about a double chin, like it's an offence worse than murder to ever get one. The tendons in her neck stand up under her skin like witch's fingers, like a handful of sticks.

"What?"

"If you find matches, or a lighter, and you put them to anything, *anything* in this house, I swear to God I'll—"

"You'll what?" I said.

"I'll kill you."

It was her fault. I pictured her collapsed and wailing by a heap of burning treasure and I couldn't stop smiling. She started it.

"What's so funny?" she asked me.

"Now you're just putting ideas into my head," I said.

Ten

Back home, before we left everything behind in such a hurry, Hannah's closet was filled to bursting with all her best things: her skirts and handbags, her elaborate, wire-boned underwear, and all of her spike-heeled, angry-looking shoes. More than half her debts probably occupied the shelves and hangers in that thing, walk-in proof of her compulsive shopping habit, her addiction to plastic, serotonin and sky-high rates of interest. She tended that closet like you would a garden. She lavished more attention on those few square feet than she'd ever mustered up for me. What can I say? It went up in flames like it was born to, like it had only ever wanted to burn all along.

It wasn't spite. I didn't plan it. It was the first time I lit a fire because things got beyond my control. I don't remember having any say in the matter. I don't recall there being a choice.

She and Lowell were throwing a lunch party for some hotshot media couple, a casting director and an agent, I think, something like that, some supposedly irresistible combination of power. They'd been planning it for months, like it might actually amount to something. Lowell couldn't get enough of grabbing me by the arm and telling me in a hushed kind of shout how important this was, how make or break career-wise. And I got it. I'm not all bad. Awkwardness aside, I was willing to try.

They brought their Neanderthal teenage son with them, Jesse, so it was my job to look after him. When they showed up, everyone got a drink and Jesse was tall and broad and charm and politeness and straight teeth. He said "yes, sir" and "no, ma'am" like some perfect, cherry-pie-eating, football-playing all-American dreamboat. Hannah was quite taken with him. I could see that. She has a better smile for the attractive ones, however old or young they might be. She looks up at them so you can see the low whites of her eyes.

Everyone was getting on fine in a fake kind of way and after a while Jesse asked to see my room.

"Good idea," said Hannah, biting into the surface of

her ice-cold vodka. "You youngsters go ahead and get acquainted."

On the way up the stairs, I told him there wasn't much to look at, and Jesse pulled a fat joint out of his pocket and smiled.

He said, "I'm sure we'll stay entertained."

We smoked the joint and my head felt heavy on my neck and numb like I'd stuffed it with wet cotton wool. I wanted to be out in the open air with Thurston, not shut in with this plastic-perfect jock. I took Jesse's box of matches and held on to it, as if it was the guardrail, and we were two hundred storeys up. I had a kind of shadow on me that I couldn't shake off. He looked at me and laughed and laughed.

It turns out we had very different ideas of what entertainment meant. After ten minutes he had me pinned under him on my single bed. His breath was sour and hot in my face and his eyes were glazed over, like he didn't even see me any more. He tore my T-shirt. He hurt my arms.

"Get off me," I said, but he didn't.

"Don't touch me," I said, but he did.

I could see my shut door from where I was lying. I shouted. I called HANNAH and HELP ME and SOMEONE PLEASE and I could hear them downstairs, I could hear their low stupid jazz and their giddy, getting-to-know-you laughter, so how come they couldn't hear me? When Jesse started undoing his fly, I dug my nails into his face hard and pulled, got out from under him and ran. I locked myself quick in Hannah and Lowell's bedroom. I heard him moaning and cursing and calling me a frigid little bitch. The fire started in me then. I felt it ignite. My parents were downstairs pinning their hopes, networking like crazy, playing host like the rest of their lives depended on it, and I knew they'd already failed, because of me. That bastard Jesse would go in bleeding, and make up some story, and the whole thing would be over before it was really begun. They hadn't even served the food yet.

I went into Hannah's closet to hide. I listened. It was dark and quiet and my heart was pounding in my ears like bass from a speaker. Jesse must have gone down around then, because I heard a scream and raised voices, and Hannah's footsteps on the stairs.

I still had Jesse's matchbox. I shook it and the matches ratcheted up against one end and then the other. I pushed it a little way open and touched them where they were sleeping, then I tipped them into the palm of my hand and counted them one by one. There were twenty. Ask anyone who's interested, twenty matches is a *find*, twenty fires if you don't waste any and you pay attention to what you're doing.

Hannah was storming through the top floor, swearing and slamming things, looking for me. She tried the door of her bedroom. I heard the handle rattle.

"Get out here, Iris," she said. "Get out here and explain yourself."

I stayed where I was.

"He touched me," I said, and I expected her to at least get it, but she didn't.

"He *what*?"

"He hurt me," I said.

"Don't be ridiculous," Hannah said through the door. "Come out right now and say sorry."

I held on to that first match a little while before I struck it. I didn't put the light on. I folded myself up in the dark and the quiet, bringing my breath back down to normal, feeling the weight of the match hardly there in my hand, rubbing the tip with my thumb. When I brought it down on the side of the box it sparked fast, orange-white, and then it flamed up bright and lit my skin a deep golden yellow in the gloom. I held on to it as long as I could while the spent end glowed and then dimmed, black and withered and done. One delicate curl of smoke furled upwards like an opening fern when I dropped it.

"Are you listening to me, Iris?" she said.

"No," I told her, my mouth pressed up against the wall.

I did it again. The smell of the second match was like hot sun and brimstone and dust and autumn leaf. There was a space at the base of the flame, a little wavering hollow and I couldn't take my eyes off it. It was that silence and emptiness I craved, the absence at the heart of it. I wanted to climb right in. Nobody would think to bother me in there.

My mother didn't let up. She told me I was selfish and ungrateful and unhinged. The longer I stayed quiet the more toxic she got. She said a lot of things through that door, but I didn't satisfy her with an answer.

It was the seventh or eighth match that I held to the net hem of one of her dresses. It went up like touch paper and in less than half a minute, Hannah's rack of clothes was raging. The paint on the closet wall started to blister. The harder it burned the less angry I got, the quieter it was in my head. I came out slowly. I shut the door and watched smoke pumping itself through all the cracks and spaces it could find, in a great rush to get out into the room. The flames started coming with it, feasting on my mother's possessions, devouring her closet from the inside out.

"Iris?" she screamed, banging on the door with her fists. "What's going on?"

I pulled the bedroom door open and walked straight past her like she wasn't there. The smoke rolled out of the room. The glass in her hand fell and bounced against the skirting, trailing droplets of vodka like tears. She said SHIT and WHAT THE? and OH MY GOD, IRIS, JESUS CHRIST and then Lowell came running. The two of them filled jugs and bowls with tap water and flung them at the fire. They drowned towels and blankets in the shower and dragged them down the hall to throw on to the flames. They were all activity and repetition, like a panicked hive. I didn't help. I didn't want to put my fire out. I wanted it to burn and burn.

When it was done, they took turns wailing and yelling until I stopped hearing them, until there was no air left in the room for the sound to carry.

At some point, the power couple took their darling boy home. They saw themselves out before anyone could stop them. Jesse got away with it. Hannah was too busy crying in the wreckage of her stupid outfits, her Louboutins and her Ungaro and her Donna Fucking Karan.

"You might have killed us all," she said, fists full of ruined fabric.

Lowell had his head in his hands. He'd already turned that almost-lunch into the mythic, one clear chance of his acting career. He'd already decided it would be my fault now, if he didn't make it.

He asked me what the hell I was thinking. I picked at a hole in my shorts and I didn't bother to tell him that the beauty of it was that I hadn't been thinking at all. That's the thing about a good fire. It empties your head completely. It razes everything to the ground so there's nothing left. It's the very definition of calm.

I took in the stench and the smoke and the soaked carpet and the ruined, irreplaceable clothes and the great smouldering wound of a closet and I couldn't shake the feeling that it was worth it. I knew I would have done it all again.

That night, instead of sleeping, I thought about rage and what else I might like to burn to the ground. I thought about Jesse, trapped in a building, with all the exits blocked, eaten alive by flames. I wished for an inferno wherever he was, harder than I'd wished for anything else in my simmering, sad little life.

And early in the morning, while Hannah and Lowell

were still sleeping it off downstairs, I went into their damp and blackened room with my old paint set and I painted an eye on the window, the pupil small and black, the eyeball white and the iris as close as I could get it to the colour of fire, like someone staring into a flame. When I left the house to look for Thurston, it watched me. It followed me all the way down the street. It didn't blink.

Eleven

The first night Hannah and I were alone here, the day Lowell left, I got called into Ernest's room very late. Lisa the night nurse crept in to get me.

"Who's that?" I said, sitting up in the dark.

"He's asking for you, Iris."

"Me? Where's my mother? Can't she go?"

She said Ernest didn't want her there, only me.

In his room, Ernest held on to my hand like he'd fallen into quicksand and I was the one pulling him out. He said there were things he hadn't explained yet. He said he needed to unburden himself and I thought, oh here we go, he's going to get it all off his chest and dump it on mine.

"Do you have to?" I said, and he seemed to think about it. I gave him some credit for that.

I stayed quiet. I thought it was the smart thing to do. I tried to make a list in my head of places I'd rather be. 1. With Thurston. 2. The airport. 3. The Grand Canyon. 4. The middle of the ocean. 5. Mars.

There were tulips from the garden in a vase by Ernest's bed. Thurston told me once there was a time centuries ago when tulips were worth more than their weight in gold, when a man would trade one single bulb for his whole house and all of its contents, would risk his life and liberty just to own it.

"It's nuts," he said, "how easily we lose our minds over stuff, how quickly money eats the world up, just like fire."

I thought about fire eating up Ernest's house, the heavy dark furniture and the curtains and the paintings and the dust. I thought about a bright flame wiping it clean and then I realised he was talking to me.

"It's all yours," he was saying. "All of it. It's all for you."

"Are we talking about money?" I said, and he looked kind of guilty.

"I'm not interested in money," I told him. "It's not why I came. I keep telling everyone that."

"Why did you come?" Ernest asked and I told him the truth.

"My mother made me. I didn't have a choice."

I heard something in the hall. Someone was outside the door listening, and I knew who it was. I could hear her breathing. It pulled at my skin like goose bumps, the quiet sound Hannah made, trying to make no sound at all.

Ernest heard it too, I was sure of it, but he carried on, louder than before.

"Not money, paintings. And the house, of course. I'd like you to have the paintings and the house."

"Ernest," I said, but he didn't hear me.

"No death duties," he said, "no stealth taxes. Everything is in a trust for when you're eighteen. I've only been looking after it."

I got up and opened the door. I could smell her perfume. I could hear her bare feet, soft on the boards of the hall. I knew she'd just been there. I knew she'd heard.

"Hannah wants your money," I said. "Not me."

He looked at me then like he was seeing me for the first time, like he hadn't really looked at me before.

"I've never loved anybody the way I loved you," he said, and it shocked me, the way he just came out with it. It made me want to curl up in a tight ball, like a louse.

It made me want to hide. My face was hot like an ember.

"I don't think I believe you," I said.

He looked angry and frail. "I haven't done it well. I've failed, and it's been an exhausting, vicious, lonely, overwhelming thing."

I didn't want to feel sorry for him but I did and it made me kind of furious. "I can't do this," I said, and I pulled my hand free of his and I got up to go.

"Do you remember anything," he said, "about me?"

"No."

"You've got me all wrong, Iris."

"No, Ernest, I haven't got you at all."

It was the middle of the night, for God's sake. I was tired and all I wanted to do was be somewhere else and be with Thurston. I wasn't ready for this. I hadn't asked for any of it.

"Lies," he said. "So many damn lies. I just want you to know the truth. I just need you to listen."

"OK," I said, but I stayed where I was, by the door, watching. "So tell me about you and my mum. Why were you ever together? How the hell did that happen in the first place?"

Twelve

Ernest tripped on a paving stone. He fell like a tree right in front of my mother in an Oxford side street. He fell, and the skin on his nose hit something sharp and burst right open. He said there was a lot of blood. Hannah helped him to sit up with his back against the window of an antique shop, his legs out in front of him on the pavement.

"That surprises me," I said. "The Hannah Baxter I know and love would have walked straight past you."

Ernest's eyes were glazed and exhausted. "Perhaps she hadn't turned into her yet."

He said it took him a minute to remember the rumpled suit trousers and the scuffed brogues he was looking at were his. There was a fine set of wine glasses in the window behind him, fanciful and delicate, with slender glass ladies for stems. They might have been dancing around his head like fairies, like stars in a cartoon. He said that's what it must have looked like to her. He turned to see what she could see, the blood still welling from the bridge of his nose.

"Handmade," he said through his darkening hand-kerchief. "1920s. Probably French."

Hannah smiled. "I'm sure I would drop one."

"Pretty pricey. Couple of hundred quid a pop."

"I could live on that for a month."

My mother's eyes were the colour of sand and envelopes, Ernest said. She was bundled up against the cold, a scarf over her mouth and chin, a hat pulled down low, an oversized coat. He couldn't see anything of her at first but her brown-paper eyes and her thin, pale hands.

Thurston showed me some photos a while ago, extreme close-ups of the human eye. They were like the surface of planets, those pictures, like whole worlds and the skin of rope and the mouths of volcanoes. I know the colour of my mother's eyes. They would have looked like deserts, sand dunes caving in on themselves in ceaseless winds. Ernest said he would have been happy to wander in them forever. I said her eyes were about as hospitable as a desert too, and he wouldn't have wandered happily for long without water, or a camel, or someone to save him.

When the ambulance came up the street for him, Ernest was embarrassed. He didn't want any fuss. He wanted to know who'd called for one, but they wouldn't say. He felt horribly visible. He knew people were watching from behind their curtains.

"Would you take me home?" he asked her.

"I can't," Hannah shook her head. He saw that her coat was stained and worn thin at the elbows. Her mouth was as pale as her skin. "I don't have a car."

"You could drive mine." He patted his bruised face. It was beginning to swell. "I'm having trouble seeing past my own nose."

He didn't tell her that home was almost two hours away. He wasn't ready for her to say no. One of the paramedics asked Hannah if she was responsible for him and so Ernest answered for her. He said that she was.

"It was my doing," he told me, "all of it."

They walked slowly to his 1946 Bentley, iron grey, sleek as a cat. She was taller than him, and thin as a rake. When he put his hand on her back to show her the way, he could feel the hard knuckles of her spine. He said Hannah raised her eyebrows at the car. She ran her fingers along its flanks like it was a living thing. Before she tried to start the engine, she took off her hat. Her long dark hair filled the car with its scent and made him dizzy. There were holes in her clothes, some badly mended, some not. She wore no make-up. She gripped the steering wheel until the bones in her hands showed white.

"It doesn't sound like her at all," I said.

"She was different then," he told me. "She had nothing to lose."

Ernest asked Hannah to tell him something about herself. She said there was nothing to tell.

"Where do you live?" he said.

"Other people's sofas."

"What do you do?" he said, and she shrugged instead of answering. The silence wasn't something she felt obliged to fill.

She crossed and uncrossed her long legs. Ernest said he tried his best not to look at them. He'd been to the Ashmolean Museum to see the world's largest collection of Raphael drawings. He'd traced each line of each drawing in his mind, from one end to the other, but he couldn't reach his usual hypnotic state. Other people kept breaking his concentration. Students and couples and pensioners, having a day out, lost in conversation, just glancing at the art. Now here he was in a trance, in his own car, with this lean girl and her long limbs, fluid as a Boldini portrait, and her eyes on him while he waited for her to speak.

Hannah wound down her window and let in the winter air. The wind was blowing in from the Arctic, the weather people had said. It had passed through Svalbard and Norway and the Faroe Islands on its way to them in their dot on the landscape, that parking space. That's all Ernest could think about, that and her legs and her hair.

She started the thing first time. "Where to?"

"It's a long way," he confessed. "It's this side of a hundred miles."

Hannah smiled. "Will you buy me lunch?" she said, and he nodded.

"If you like."

"I don't have anywhere else to be."

They stopped at a pub and she ate like she hadn't eaten in a while, like she wasn't sure where her next meal was coming from. She was starving, he realised. And after she'd eaten, he drove so she could sleep, and he tried to keep his eyes on the road.

At the house, he showed her around. He pulled out all the stops: his dad's vintage cars, his art collection. My mother took it all in.

"This has got to be worth *millions*," she cooed, putting her perfect upturned nose against the cold skin of a Picasso Blue Nude.

She spent the night in one of the guest rooms. It hadn't been slept in for years. They uncovered the antique rosewood furniture, the bed and chest and dressing table. The air swam with dust that gathered in the space around them like plankton around whales. Ernest had a sneezing fit and the skin on his nose broke open and bled again. He sat in a delicate, high-backed chair and pressed the wound shut while Hannah put fresh sheets on the bed.

In the morning, half asleep, he strolled into the kitchen in his pyjamas as usual. Hannah was standing at the door with her back to him, looking out over the frosty garden. Ernest could feel the heat coming off her from twenty feet away. The sky was grey and it seemed to him that there was no sign of life out there, nothing at all, except for her. He asked her to stay. He said it out loud before he could think his way out of it. He was tired of being alone. He wanted to live a little, like Margot had told him. My mother smiled. He expected her to decline politely, to ask him to call her a cab, but she didn't.

She was twenty-one and he was her ticket out of nowhere.

Thurston is twenty-one now too. I missed his birthday. He must have thought my heart was a piece of flint, a small sharp scrap of cold stone. He helped me make a timeline once of things achieved by people at different ages. I know twenty-one off by heart. When he was twenty-one, Arthur Rimbaud abandoned poetry forever. Billy the Kid was shot dead at the OK Corral. Sylvia Plath made her first suicide attempt, stealing her mother's pills and lying in the crawl space under the house for three whole days before she was found.

Ernest was thirty-three. Mary Wollstonecraft wrote *Vindication of the Rights of Women* at thirty-three. Ralph Waldo Emerson wrote his essay "Nature", encouraging us to see the miraculous in the everyday. Ernest saw the miraculous in my mother, or at least he thought he did. Proof again, I suppose, that we see what we want to see, regardless of what we are actually looking at, nothing at all to do with the truth.

Hannah never collected her things. Ernest didn't even know if she had any. He didn't meet anyone from her life before, not at the beginning. She started from scratch, like she was brand-new. He had the antique shop in Oxford send the set of glasses, special delivery. Hannah opened the parcel and kissed him. Then she dropped one on the flagstone floor of the kitchen.

"She did it on purpose," he told me, "because they were hers now, because she could."

Thirteen

Ernest didn't have much time left, but he seemed to have time enough for me. I didn't mind when he thought I was his sister, and at some point I stopped minding that this was all about dealing with his own guilt. I stopped minding and I started to enjoy it while it lasted. He was pretty good company, even when he slipped away on the pain meds and you almost lost him. Even then he had stuff to say that I was interested in hearing.

He slept a lot. And then sometimes he was clearer than others, all there in the room, wide awake and pin sharp, like none of him was sick or weak or missing. He looked out of his big picture windows, like giant screens where he got to watch live footage of the world. The pale backs of leaves dancing in the last of the sun, the quick fact of a bird on the ledge, low planes overhead, the turned earth in furrowed lines in the fields beyond the garden. Ordinary things, I suppose, but not if you were Ernest, and time was running out, and you didn't know how many chances you'd get to see those things again.

I told him that soon we'd all be able to choose the view from our houses. Soon, our windows would open on to all possible virtual worlds and we'd move ourselves from desert island to mountain-top to outer space at the touch of a button.

"And how will we do that?" he said.

"Nano-transformational technology," I said. "Holograms, I suppose."

"Really?" he said. "In your lifetime?"

"It won't be long," I told him. "Our cars will look like limousines to us if we want them to, a new model, a different colour every day. Our roads will be empty, sunlit highways, whatever it is we are driving on, whatever jalopy we drive."

"How so?" he said, and I liked the way he said it. It made me smile.

"Three-dimensional projections," I said. "Hyper-real, interactive illusions."

"Fakes?" he said and he laughed.

"Yes, fakes," I said. "The real won't be real enough any more. Only appearances will count."

"Imagine that," he said. "Hannah and Lowell will fit right in."

"Children will be born," I told him, "who'll have no idea that the holograms aren't real because the holograms will be real, to them. In the end, everyone who remembers a time without them will be dead."

"And what use are the dead to the living?" said Ernest. "They don't even speak the same language."

"You talk to Margot often enough," I said.

"Do I?" He looked surprised. "Must be because I'm nearly there."

Ernest knew he wouldn't be around to see it happen. He'd lived through the beginning of a revolution but he wouldn't see the end. He said he'd try not to judge.

"I've performed my fair share of illusions," he said, "after all."

Still, if he looked out at the night sky through his window and compared it to some future virtual digital recording of the night sky through his window, he wasn't all that sorry to be going.

"In the face of all this mastery of wonder," he said, "I long to rise and glide out, to paraphrase Walt Whitman, to wander off by myself, and from time to time look up in perfect silence at the stars."

"Walt Whitman?" I said.

"Yes. Read him. Read him soon, before I'm gone and the nano-transformers have taken over. Read him in a real-life, actual, rare as hen's teeth *book*."

He was quiet for a while and I sort of knew what he was thinking so I told him about a thing Thurston and I used to do, a when-I'm-dead game. Thurston started it one night, out of nowhere, when we were out walking.

"When I'm dead," he said, "I'm going to become the skin of an antler, the root of a tooth."

"Can I be an oyster shell?" I said. "The very tip of a tree?"

"We can be anything," Thurston said. "If the mass of the Universe never changes, we have to be some part of it when we die."

"Not stars," I said. "Let's not be stars. Let's be paper and subway trains and honey."

"Let's be children's shoes and paintbrushes and lint."

"When I'm dead," he said, "I'm going to take up smoking."

I smiled. "I suppose it can't hurt."

"I'll drive too fast and jump out of aeroplanes and eat blowfish and toadstools and beach apples. I'll do my best to drink too much and never ever look before I cross the road."

I joined in. "When I'm dead I'll wear highly flammable clothing and live in a volcano and jump off high buildings and walk across waterfalls on a tightrope."

"We'll be fearless skydivers."

"And swim in shark-infested waters."

"I might join an expedition to the North Pole in a T-shirt."

"I'll join a circus and team up with a blind knife thrower."

"I'm almost looking forward to it," Thurston said.

"Don't say that," I told him. "You don't mean that."

When I told Ernest to give it a go, he looked at me for a minute.

"When I'm dead, I will probably sit at my kitchen table with an infinite pack of my old French cigarettes and watch you, whatever it is you're doing."

I laughed. "That's it?" I said. "A whole world of possibilities and you want to stay here and look at me?"

"Do you think you'll know if I'm here?" Ernest said. "Maybe you'll smell my tobacco. It's strangely delicious, like burnt leaves and dung."

"Nice."

"If you do, you must look over. You have to say hello."

"What will you say?"

"Oh, nothing much. I'll complain about the lack of good brandy in paradise."

"Paradise? Is that where you're going? Are you sure about that?"

"My wings are still small," he said, smiling and shifting in the bed. "They feel like fists under my skin. They're not ready yet, but they're coming."

Then he asked me if I'd stay here, after he was gone.

"You don't have to," he said. "You can do what you want. Sell the place."

"I won't sell your house, Ernest."

"Your house."

"Whatever," I told him. "I don't know yet. But I do like it here."

I hadn't thought about what would happen when he was gone. I said so.

"Well you need to," he said. "That's what's happening. I'm going."

"I know," I said. "You're going. I get it."

Ernest sighed. "And you only just got here."

He'd patrol the grounds while I slept, he said, and check the locks and passages and stairwells for other ghosts and intruders. He'd sit high in the branches of a tree and listen to the night birds, and the cars that sounded as they passed like waves on a beach, coming in close and then falling away.

"I won't leave this place if I can help it," he told me. "Not if you're in it. I don't think I could."

"But you left me my whole life until now," I said, and then I regretted it, because it sounded mean and bitter, even if it was true.

He shook his head. "No," he said.

"Yes, Ernest. Do me a favour. Don't say you'll always be here and crap like that because it's cheap."

"I'm sorry."

"Don't sugar-coat the tiny piece of you I *am* getting," I said.

"OK."

"And don't make promises you can't keep," I said. "I don't like it. It's not right."

He leaned forward a little, closer to me. "Have I told you about *Fire Colour One*?"

It was the first time he mentioned it. I'm sure about that.

"*Fire Colour One*?" I said. "The Yves Klein painting?"

"Shhh!" He put his hand out. "Not so loud."

"What about it?"

"How much do you know? What have I said?"

"Nothing," I told him. "You haven't said anything. I know what it is, that's all. I know it well."

"You do?"

Thurston had a thing about Yves Klein. I said so. Yves Klein was important, according to him, a visionary, daring and tragic, and ahead of his time.

"For a start, he owned the sky," I said.

Ernest looked out of the window at the low grey. "He did?"

"Yes. When he was a kid, he and his friends lay on a beach and divided the elements between them. He got the sky."

"Lucky boy," Ernest said.

"Proper genius, according to Thurston."

We'd got into the USC Library with fake ID cards (I was 107, Thurston was 93) and he read to me about Klein's *Zones of Immaterial Pictorial Sensibility*. I didn't get it. He had to explain.

"Basically, he got people to pay him gold bullion for nothing."

"Nothing?"

"Well, no, for something, for a moment, for empty space," Thurston said. "He gave them a receipt for it. But if they burnt that, he chucked half the gold bullion in the Seine for them too."

"And kept the other half," I said.

"It's brilliant, isn't it?" Thurston said. "It's genius."

I grinned at him. "Not publicity-hungry commercialism then."

"You know what?" Thurston told me. "There was nobody like him. Not then. He couldn't be copied."

"Surely everything can be copied."

"Well Yves Klein couldn't," Thurston said. "How could anyone copy him when he didn't even touch his own canvasses?"

"What?"

"It says here, *He kept a defined and constant distance from the works of art that he created.*"

"Who painted them then," I asked, "if he didn't?"

Thurston showed me the book, old photos from the sixties.

"His models," Thurston said. "They were his brushes. They were his orchestra. He invited an audience. And he conducted."

"He got pretty girls to cover their naked bodies in paint and press themselves against things," I said. "You're right, Thurston. He was a genius."

"He looked into the void," he said, and I rolled my eyes.

"Whatever that means."

"He invented a colour," he told me. "International Klein Blue. He trademarked it."

"I'll bet he did."

"He covered canvasses with solid, uninterrupted colour. The same size canvasses, the same colour, with different price tags, because they were different moments of creation."

"Ha! How do you know the man wasn't a charlatan?"

Thurston smiled his most open smile that meant I knew half as much as I thought I did but he still liked me anyway.

"Because he brought art out of the airless studio and back to life. He made it immediate. He made it into something more than escape, more than the prison window. He made it exciting and real. He used time and space and wind and rain and fire. He strapped a canvas to the roof of his car and drove to the beach and let the weather make his art for him."

"The prison window," I said. "I like that."

"Look," said Thurston, "here's one for you. *Fire Colour One.*"

The scorched outline of two women, their arms outstretched, like dancers, primitive and elemental.

I looked at it for a long time. I turned the page and there were more photos, black and white and still bristling with something intense, and not thought of, and new.

"How do you paint with fire?" Thurston said.

"With a blowtorch to start with," I showed him, "and then a bloody great gas-powered fire cannon."

I told Ernest that Yves Klein died suddenly in 1962 when he was only 34. His friends thought he had burned himself up and left nothing but a great vacuum. He was a comet, someone said, whose path through life was traced by the scorched empty space he left behind.

Just before he died, he announced that he would only produce "immaterial works" from that point onward, and afterwards, people thought he must have known that he was about to become immaterial, about to join the ranks of the dead. They had no other explanation for it than that.

Ernest listened to me intently the whole time I was talking. He didn't take his eyes off me for a second.

"I'm glad you know a little about art," he said, "and the great man."

I shrugged. "I know what Thurston taught me."

"Imagine knowing when you're going to die," Ernest said to me then, and I swear there was a new light in his eyes, a quick glimmer. "Just imagine what you would do."

Fourteen

After I destroyed the closet, after the landlord had threatened to evict us, someone told Hannah and Lowell that I had to get a trip to the fire station. They marched me down there, barking like dogs, hauled me up in front of the first fireman they could find, whose name was Collins, the uncle of a boy I knew at school.

"I made an appointment," Hannah said, like that was a proper substitute for "Hello".

He shifted on his feet. "We usually do groups," he said, "class visits, not individual children."

"She's home-schooled," said Lowell, which was a lie, but convincing enough, especially with the $20 bill he showed him. "Make an exception."

*

Thurston made beautiful banknotes with Miles Davis and Rosa Parks and Mark Twain on them, with Jenny Holzer slogans (PROTECT ME FROM WHAT I WANT) and a Lawrence Weiner quote (THEY DON'T HAVE TO BUY IT TO HAVE IT – THEY CAN JUST HAVE IT BY KNOWING IT). He had this idea that they'd go into local circulation. He wanted to start a micro-economy, collective and anti-capitalist, something generous and better and new.

"Even if it's just a few streets," he said, "it would be something, wouldn't it?"

At the fire station, I could see Andrew Jackson's face on Lowell's $20, the seventh President of the United States, a slave trader, by the way, who engineered genocide against the Native American people, and profited from the repossession of their land. Maybe it's an honour a man like that doesn't deserve, but then again sometimes I think the best place for him is stuck on the back of a twenty for all eternity. The guy must have really loved money. Lowell palmed it like a dealer and passed it over in a handshake. He got a kick out of doing that, I could tell.

Officer Collins had a short brown beard, thick and blunt-cut like a doormat, and huge red hands like cuts of meat. At the sound of my mother's voice, three or four other firemen had wandered out into the yard from the back room. They stood like his back line and watched. He took the money, pocketed it, looked at Lowell and nodded.

"Five minutes," he said.

Hannah yanked me into place.

"These men," she yelled, "are going to tell you what's what. So help me God, you'd better be listening."

They went to wait in the car, Hannah's sandals slapping across the yard like flat hands. Officer Collins kept his eyes on the ground. I'm not sure he appreciated my family's feel for drama. Either that or he knew I'd just seen how much he cost. He smiled at me, smoothed his wire-haired face down from top to bottom, and sighed, "Let's go."

I followed him down a lightless corridor that smelled of old trainers and rubber and sweat.

"Fire is not a game," he said over his shoulder and I nodded and tried to keep my face straight. I was too old for this. "A small fire can grow into a deadly fire in one or two minutes."

He told me these things the same way I used to practise my spelling from start to finish, without thinking, because I'd done it a thousand times before, because I had to.

I could have been anyone. Officer Collins didn't seem to care.

"Never play with matches or lighters or petrol," he said. I wondered why he thought I was playing with any of it at all.

He showed me all the equipment, the suits and masks hanging empty, the idle flat hose, the stacked-up breathing apparatus, the parked truck. It was a disappointment, frankly. There was next to nothing going on. The firemen that I saw were watching TV, playing cards, killing time. I wondered if they ever wanted a fire to happen, the same way I did, just for something to break the monotony, just for something to do. I had my fingers crossed behind my back that the alarms would sound, that they'd leap up like superheroes, that I'd get to see them in action, but they didn't, I didn't. They stayed slumped at tables, catnapping on couches, scratching, smoking and eating. It smelled of burnt bacon and gas in there.

Officer Collins gave me a bunch of sad leaflets. They said MEET BUZZY THE SMOKE DETECTOR! and I'M SPLASH THE FIRE EXTINGUISHER! They said NEVER COOK IN LONG SLEEVES! and WHY NOT PRACTISE YOUR OWN FIRE DRILL? I pictured myself putting a match underneath them. I imagined them flowering to ash in my hand. I'd have liked to give him some leaflets of my own. DON'T PATRONISE A PYROMANIAC!! DON'T UNDERESTIMATE A QUIET KID WITH A LIGHTER!!! DON'T SPEND THAT $20 ON FRIED MEAT, FATSO!!

Back out in the yard, he put his face level with mine. Up close, I could see the tiny holes in his skin where the hairs grew, like wet clay pushing through a sieve.

He said, "Young lady, I hear you had some trouble with a fire."

I shrugged. "I don't know. It was an accident. It was no trouble."

He looked at the sky and laughed. I could see where his teeth had gone brown, right at the back of his mouth.

"I'm going to make a deal with you," he said. "If you don't strike a match or play with fire for the next two weeks, if you can come back and say you haven't done it, then you can go with us in the fire truck, if you'd like to."

I didn't say anything. I rolled my eyes at him. I wasn't a stupid kid any more.

"Wouldn't you like to?" he said.

I shook my head. "Not so much."

"Haven't you ever thought about being a fire fighter yourself?"

I stared him out.

"You see a lot of fires that way," Officer Collins leaned back a little, like a fisherman, reeling me in. "You get up real close. You do it again and again and again."

I kept my mouth shut. I wore my poker face and when Hannah and Lowell called me over, I walked slow and steady to the car.

Two weeks is a long time to go without a thing when you have a proper thirst for it. The whole world was tempting me to fail, leaving cigarettes burning in ashtrays, matches on the sidewalk, dropping lighters from pockets, from bags. Everywhere I looked there was a trap someone had set for me, like they'd read the stupid safety leaflets and decided to do the exact opposite. But that fire truck was waiting, scrubbed and shined and gleaming, just around the corner. I told Thurston. I said it was worth trying for and I was going to try damn hard. I wanted to speed through the streets in that thing, its siren wailing, its bulk shifting underneath me, its lights flashing danger and rescue all at once. If I was one of them, I could get as close to a fire as I dared and it would be OK, it'd be my job. I'd get paid for it, and get up every morning and do it again. For two long weeks I ignored the matches and the cigarette butts and the naked flames. For fourteen days and nights I sat on my hands and didn't try to find out what a box of dolls looked like on fire, or a shoe, or a stack of magazines left out with the trash, damp and mottled with bat shit. I walked past all of those things with my face turned away. And when it was over, I went back down to the fire station. Nobody needed to march me there this time. I was glad to go.

There was still nothing much happening. They were all still lolling about like fed dogs, time-wasting, cooking sausages, dozing. It was like Sleeping Beauty's castle in there. Officer Collins didn't even get up off his butt and he wouldn't look at me either, not straight on. He cleared his throat in his big old easy chair and said that they were extremely busy and they didn't have time to drive one home-schooled kid around that day, no way.

He said, "What's your name again?"

I glared at him. "Iris."

"That's right," he said. "Iris. Did you get caught smoking? Was that you?"

"No," I told him. "I don't smoke."

He shrugged. "Come by next open day and maybe you can climb up inside and take a look."

"What's this now?" one of the others asked him.

I told him. I said we had a deal that I could ride in the truck.

He laughed, punching Collins on the arm. "You gotta stop that, Joe. How many kids you promised this month?"

Collins grinned. "I lost count."

It didn't matter what I said. He wasn't keeping his promise, however hard I'd worked to keep mine. A ride in a fire truck didn't seem to mean a thing to him, one way or the other. Like the saying goes, you don't know what you've got until it's gone.

Thurston was waiting for me when I got home. He was sitting on the wall outside my apartment building.

"How'd it go?" he said.

I looked at him. "They lied to me," I said. "I don't want to talk about it."

I left him there on the wall and I went inside and sulked in my room. I could hear the neighbours' washed sheets snapping outside like sails in the wind. It was a hot dry day and it hadn't rained in a while. I lay on my bed and listened to the sirens in my head. Any minute, I was going to get up, get a few things together, sneak out and light the mother of all fires, fourteen days' worth, behind the tiny parched yard out back. Nobody would see me. I was going to light three, starting in the far corner and moving in. The wind would pick them up and pull them together and I'd be back inside by the time anyone noticed a thing. Those sheets would be grey with soot before they could get them in.

I was still lying there when Thurston came round the back of the building and threw a handful of stones against my window. The sirens in my head were suddenly real, suddenly outside. I looked out and he bowed, like a man on a stage, and offered me the view with a sweep of his arm. What I'd been thinking about, Thurston had been doing, quiet as a cat. That dried-out stretch of land was leaping, wild red and crackling, the heat coming off it like surf, flames lapping against the garages and summerhouses, pooling at the edge of the ground-floor properties. I don't know how many people had dialled 911. Their phones must have been ringing off the hook. I stood at my window and watched the fire trucks come, more than one, sirens on, lights blazing, filled to the brim with superheroes dressed in hard hats and fat trousers and bug-eyed masks. I stayed out of sight and I watched those lazy, good-for-nothing, promise-breaking, bacon-crammed firemen as they battled with the flames. Nobody was hurt. They lost a couple of verandas to the fire, and an old disused pick-up, and someone's trellis, someone else's doghouse. They lost a few gallons in sweat, I'd say, as well, and maybe a pound or two in weight.

Thurston stood behind the barrier, watching with the rest of the small crowd, blending in, wearing just the right mask of shock and awe on his face.

THANK YOU, I mouthed at him through the glass when he looked up.

He blew me a kiss. YOU'RE WELCOME, it said.

Fifteen

Ernest said that the tree outside his window arrived years ago from Holland, on Margot's twelfth birthday. A black pear, already twenty feet high, more than eight feet around, he said its root ball alone weighed almost three tonnes. The men stopped on the road with it strapped down like Gulliver in the bed of their lorry. Passing drivers slowed to make sense of what they were seeing, caught a glimpse of the felled giant, and then were gone.

"We ran outside," he said, "and there it was, a tree on its side, made from ravens and dragons, its thick bark crackled with scales, the buds of its leaves smooth and solid as claws."

They invaded the tree like termites. Their mum watched with her arms folded and her mouth in a thin straight line before she called them inside and scolded them for playing near the road.

Margot fumed.

"But it's a lying-down tree," she said.

"And it's Margot's birthday," Ernest added. "We thought it was for her."

She didn't soften. She sent them upstairs to wash their hands and think about what they'd done.

"What would you do with your own tree anyway?" Ernest asked.

"Climb it," Margot said. "Carve my name in it with a knife, lean against its trunk in the shade, eat its fruit." She sighed. "So much better than a doll."

He said she'd slouched into the nursery that morning trailing the new doll after her, bumping it along the floorboards. She'd dragged the thing in by its long corn-yellow hair.

"What am I going to do with this?" she asked.

Ernest sniggered. "Tie it to some train tracks," he suggested. "Shoot it with arrows. Gouge out its eyes and fill its head with birdseed."

Margot grinned. "Drown it in a cattle trough," she said. "Set fire to its hair."

And then the tree came, he said, and the doll was forgotten, left on the floor with one eye shut and its polka-dot dress pulled up over its head while the children pressed their faces flat against the windows to get a better view.

He sat up in bed and looked out while he told me.

"The crane driver sat in his cab," he said, pointing, "and when the tree lifted, it came up head first and then hung just there, strangely upright, like it was planted in mid-air."

It cast a shadow over all the rooms they ran through, a great dark beast flying past the house. It blocked out the sun, the birds stopped singing and downstairs someone dropped a plate on the flagstone floor.

The men dug a crater on the east side of the house, a great bowl of a scar, the turf cut open and pulled back over itself like so much skin. Ernest said it looked as if the moon had fallen right out of the sky and landed in their garden. Margot wanted more than anything to crouch at the bottom of that hole and look up at the sky. She saw herself out there in the cool, upturned earth, like buried treasure. She would open out, she said, with her spine pressed into the ground like a worm and the shadows of birds gliding across her face.

"Don't even think about it," said his mum, one hand resting on the back of Margot's neck.

"Of course it was too late," Ernest said. "She already had."

*

Thurston planted one hundred trees in unexpected places the spring before last. He'd grown all these saplings from scratch, yogurt pots and buckets filled with the things and we went around putting them outside buildings, in cracks in the sidewalk, in car parks and alleys and gas stations. We made a map so we could visit them all and water them. He wanted to start a forest in the middle of LA. Most of them got pulled up or trampled in the first week. Then he got this group of secret gardeners together, kids mostly, who snuck out in the middle of the night to dig up public spaces and plant vegetables. That whole spring, instead of paint and glue, his hands were covered in soil, but nothing lasted. He didn't get a full-grown tree like this one. He had to start with nothing, and nothing got left where it was, to grow.

Margot and Ernest weren't allowed to get their hands dirty, not that day. They sprawled across the nursery floor like late bees, dying of boredom. The tree was lying slain in the garden and the men had stopped for lunch. In a fit of caution, their mum had locked the doors. Nobody was allowed outside until the thing was staked and planted. She didn't trust the men to know what they were doing. She didn't trust it not to roll or break or fall.

Ernest's dad called her a catastrophist. He said Margot would get cabin fever, but not Ernest of course, her houseplant child, her rare orchid.

Ernest was trying to make the perfect spit bubble. Margot said it was the worst birthday ever. They lay on their backs, staring at a crack in the ceiling until their vision blurred and the crack swam about and disappeared.

Margot said, "I want to bury something. Let's hide treasure under the tree for someone to dig up in five hundred years. What have we got that's good enough?"

They packed everything neatly into a black metal box, locked it and shared out the keys: one left in the lock, to be helpful, and one above the picture rail in the nursery. Margot climbed on top of the toy cupboard to put it there. Ernest still remembered the things they'd buried like it was yesterday. While he was telling me, he looked down at his lap as if they were spread out on the bed in front of him, as if he could see them all. A pocket mirror, the front page of the newspaper, Margot's silver christening cup. Ernest's wounded toy soldiers. A photo of both of them together. A feather, an old horse medicine bottle with Ernest's baby tooth in it, and some of Margot's hair, and a drop of each of their blood. Margot cut his thumb with her whittling knife and said, "Who knows what they'll be able to tell about us in the future from these samples? They might make new ones of us altogether. We'll wake up in a lab in a thousand years and get to live our lives again."

Ernest wanted to know if he'd remember his first life, this one, when they buried the stuff.

"Probably," Margot said. "But mostly we'll remember the five hundred years of waiting under that tree."

Ernest said, "I didn't want to do that." He said he started to snivel, but Margot told him to be brave, in the interests of future science.

Work had started up again. The tree was airborne, swinging into position.

It was her idea, she said, so it should be her job to bury it.

Ernest watched from the window while Margot skipped down the back stairs, took the spare key from the hook in the kitchen and was gone.

"By the time anyone else saw her," he said, "it was almost too late."

The crane screamed in its efforts to stop the tree from crashing down on top of her. There was a great screeching of brakes and a grinding of metal on metal and then the shouts of the men got louder. Ernest said his mum ran out of the house, shrieking and tearing at her hair, white as a sheet. She looked seasick, everyone did. Only Margot looked overjoyed and defiant, beaming, her arms and legs stuck with mud as she climbed out of the crater, the tree's roots swaying like snakes in the air less than six feet above her head. Her dad slapped her face, and Ernest burst into tears, but Margot didn't stop smiling.

"Why didn't you just throw the box in?" he asked her later through her bedroom door. Margot had been sent to bed without supper. She was officially in disgrace. He'd have been in trouble just for talking to her.

"Where's the fun in that?" she said. "I had to lie down in there, the way I pictured it, or the box would have seen what I never got to see."

"A tree, coming to crush you to death?"

"Exactly," hissed Margot. "It was terrifying. It was brilliant."

"But it was so dangerous," he said. "You could've been killed."

"Haven't you worked it out yet?" Margot asked him. "What?"

"Life's big secret. If a thing's not dangerous, it's hardly worth doing."

"That can't be true," he said.

"Oh, but it is."

"Mother is going to kill you," he told her.

She was tired of the conversation. He could hear it in her voice. "Don't be silly, Ernest. That's precisely the last thing she's ever going to do. Mother is all about keeping us alive, at the expense of anyone having any actual fun."

"What does that mean?"

"Do you remember the last time we were really high up on the ridge in the wind and Mother panicked and told us all not to look down? Well, she was wrong. I looked down and the view was unbelievable."

Ernest looked at me and smiled.

"She said, 'What's the point of being up there if you're not going to look down? What's the point of doing anything at all?'"

Sixteen

Hannah watched Ernest and me pretty closely. She didn't much like us spending time together, not without her there. Guaranteed, after less than five minutes her footsteps would echo up the stairs or she'd call my name from somewhere else in the house. I wasn't used to it, my mother minding where I was. It made me feel uncomfortable.

"She's anxious about her inheritance," I said to Ernest. "You know she was listening outside the door the other night."

"Of course she was," he said. "She wouldn't be Hannah if she wasn't."

Fluid from his lungs was draining into a bag. It was the colour of mustard water, cloudy and adrift like a lava lamp. Without that bag, he'd have drowned.

"She'll be furious if you leave me everything."

"I know," he said. "She thinks it's a terrible idea."

"So give it to her," I told him. "I don't need it."

He smiled. "I'm waiting for her to persuade me."

"Really?" I said. "Good."

"She doesn't like being upstaged by her daughter."

"I'm not upstaging anyone," I said.

"Yes, you are," he said and his throat sounded thick and hoarse. "And what's worse is, you're not even trying."

"I don't want to try."

"Even more infuriating. Your mother is used to being the centre of attention."

"Lowell's worse," I said, and he looked unconvinced. "I mean it. Seriously."

I told him that Lowell spent even more time in front of a mirror than Hannah did. He was the first to wilt if nobody was looking at him, like a plant in a drought. He lasted two minutes and twenty-eight seconds in a room alone before he picked up the phone and called somebody so he could talk about himself. I knew that for a fact because I'd timed him. Two minutes twenty-eight was his personal best.

Ernest's laugh was like stones landing in a puddle. "She met her match then."

"I don't know about that." I'd always wondered what there was for her to like about Lowell, once she'd got used to his handsome, predictable face.

He said, "Have you ever met her family?"

I shook my head. "I didn't think there was any," I said. "I figured she was born out of an egg."

"They were poor," he said. "I know that much. I worked that much out for myself."

"Well she loves money well enough."

"It saved her," he said, and I told him, "Depends which way you look at it."

He said, "She never liked how you and I got on."

"Us?" I said. "You and me? Did we?"

"Like a house on fire," he said, and I tried not to blush, but felt my cheeks flaming up anyway.

"I don't remember," I told him.

"But I do," Ernest said.

He closed his eyes while the nurse shut off the tube in his side and covered it with a clean dressing. He knew what Hannah was up to, with the inventory and everything. I showed him my notebook. I hadn't paid much attention to the dining-room cabinets, but I had walked through the rooms making a list of all the art. My mother was right about one thing. Ernest's collection was incredible.

I told him. I said he must be proud of the beautiful things he'd filled his house with, centuries of them, old masters and impressionists and modernists silently preening on his walls. I said I wished Thurston could be here. He'd have been so happy to get that close without an alarm sounding, without three security guards removing him from the building. He'd tried to touch the *Mona Lisa* when he was a kid and it came to LA. He hardly moved before they stopped him, grown men with static radios and steel-cap shoes.

"It was a thought-crime," he said. "And the second time I tried, I was out. My feet didn't touch the ground."

"Do you have a favourite?" Ernest asked me, but I didn't. How was I supposed to compare them? It wasn't possible.

"But look at this," I showed him my notebook. "We're cataloguing you. I think Hannah's getting ready for the biggest yard sale of all time."

He leaned forward and pinched the bridge of his nose with his fingers.

"She's done that before," he said. "She knows what's here. She's had everything valued already."

"When?"

"Years ago. Your mother likes to be in control of things."

"No shit," I told him. "I've met her too you know."

He laughed. "And she wants to control what we talk about."

He shifted in his bed. I got up and sorted out his pillows. "Better," he whispered. "Thank you."

Ernest said she was afraid of the things he knew, things she wouldn't want him to tell me.

"Like what?"

"My story," he said. "My version of the truth."

"So why would she bring me," I said, "if she had stuff to hide?"

"Money," he said. "The prize. Don't underestimate its hold over her. Your mother will stop at nothing to get it."

"You think?" I said, smiling.

"And she didn't expect me to last this long. I don't think she planned for us to meet at all."

"True," I said. "She kind of hoped you'd be dead when we got here."

"Your mother never liked to wait for things."

"So when are you going to tell me your version?" I said. "You're going to, right? You will?"

We could hear Hannah's voice on the stairs, getting louder. "Iris? Iris! Where are you?"

"Three and a half minutes," I said. "She's getting quicker."

"You'll know everything," he said. "As soon as we get the chance."

"*Fire Colour One*," I said. "Tell me about that."

"Oh God, not now," he told me. "Not a word. Not in front of her."

My mother pushed into the room, loud and breathless, looking from me to him and back again like she'd be able to tell by our faces how much had been said.

"Jane needs you in the kitchen," she said. "That woman hasn't the first idea how to make a California roll."

"I'm coming," I said, staying right where I was. "I'll be down in a minute."

"No," she said, gripping on to the door with both hands, white-knuckled with stress and boredom and the slow passing of time. "*You'll go now*."

She was showing signs of going for too long without a copy of *Vogue* or an eyebrow wax. The polish on her nails was beginning to chip. Her hair looked kind of greasy. It was only a matter of time before she'd have to go back to the city.

"An egg you say?" Ernest said, and he winked at me and sank back into his pillows. I could see he was in pain and it occurred to me that he hadn't taken his morphine, not that I noticed, not while he was with me.

A vein in Hannah's temple was pulsing. Her eyes burnt laser holes into my sweatshirt, willing me to leave. I got up slowly, to annoy her more than anything.

"See you later," I said.

Ernest waved and Hannah and I stared each other out until she shut the door on me, shut herself in the room with him, and turned the key in the door. It occurred to me she could step up and play the grim reaper herself if she just had five minutes with him on her own. It was a terrible thing to think about my own mother, but it had the ring of truth about it all the same.

From where I was standing at the top of the stairs, I caught the faint, acid scent of burnt paper. It was there and then it was gone. I wondered if it was one of my little fires, still burning; or my own brain playing tricks on me.

I stayed where I was. I had this dumb idea about trying to protect him. If anything happened I could beat the door down or go and get Dawn. And I was curious too. I wanted to listen to what they were saying. I wondered what it was like between the two of them now, my mother and my dad.

So I deserved to hear what I did. Standing on the wrong side of that locked door in the quiet, I suddenly realised Hannah was ramping up the competition, playing me to win. And like the cage-fighter she was underneath that glossy surface, she didn't care how low down she went to do it.

Seventeen

My mother was pacing Ernest's room in her high heels, with her loping walk. Her shoes were loud as hammers on the wooden boards. I pictured her reading charts or dialling up the morphine dosage or getting ready to switch something vital off or up or around. When she finally sat down, I heard the sigh and shush of her skirt riding up, her legs crossing and uncrossing, Hannah-style, and I heard my own heartbeat, pulsing away in the quiet of the hall. I'll bet she ran her hand up and down her arm and gave him her best look too.

She did something like that, because Ernest laughed, just a little. "We're way past that, Hannah," he said. "Just tell me what you want."

"We need to talk about Iris," she said.

Ernest's breath sounded like that last little drop of

soda being pulled through a straw. "What is there to say?"

"She seems pleased to see you."

"I think we're doing OK."

"Don't be fooled," she told him, and every cell of my body went on high alert.

"By what? By Iris?"

"I don't think you can trust her."

Ernest waited. I counted to three before he said, "What is this, Hannah?"

"She's dangerous," my mother said. "She could hurt you."

I went cold all over. I wanted to bang on the door and have my say, but I didn't even move. I just stood there.

"Believe me," Ernest told her. "Nothing is getting through this morphine wall."

"You don't understand," Hannah said. "Iris isn't right."

I pressed my head against the wall and tried to breath right.

"How?" said Ernest. "What in God's name are you talking about?"

"I'm talking about arson," she whispered, like saying it any louder could make it happen.

She wasn't lying. I couldn't exactly deny it.

"Arson?"

"You can't let Iris near matches or anything like that," Hannah said.

"You're serious?"

"She'll burn the place down as soon as look at you."

"Why are you telling me this now?" Ernest said.

"I'm worried about you with her here. I can't sleep or even think straight I'm so worried about your safety."

"My safety's not really an issue," he said. "If I die tomorrow it's only a few days ahead of schedule."

"And the paintings?" she said.

"Ah," he said. "That's more like it. The paintings. They're insured, Hannah."

"They're irreplaceable," she said. "You know that."

"And?"

"And I think we should move them now."

"Where to?"

"I don't know. An auction house, proper storage. Somewhere else."

Ernest sighed. I heard him. His voice was small and flat and defeated. "I don't think we need to do that."

"If Iris starts one of her fires," Hannah told him, "we

won't get you out of here quick enough. You'll go off like a bomb with all this oxygen in the room."

I had this idea that my mother was going to torch the place and then blame it on me. It rushed through me like a blast of cold air.

"Not such a bad way to go," he told her.

"She set fire to my bedroom," Hannah said. "And our apartment block. She set fire to her school, for God's sake. She's out of control. She won't stop."

"Why didn't you say something before?" Ernest asked. "Why did you bring her here if she's such a threat?"

"You told me to," she said. "You wanted it."

I could almost taste it, his disapproval, of her or of me, I wasn't sure.

"That mattered all of a sudden, did it?" he said. "What I wanted?"

"We left the States," she told him, "because Iris burned us out. People were threatening to sue." I pictured her pinching her finger and thumb together. "She was this close to getting arrested for arson, or sectioned, or both."

Neither of them spoke. I stood still in the quiet, hardly breathing, hearing even the sound my eyelids made when I blinked. I should have told him myself. What must he think of me now?

"Do you understand what I'm saying?" said Hannah.

"She lights fires." Ernest sounded far away, like he'd been punching the morphine button.

"She's dangerous."

"What do you want from me?" he said.

Hannah stood up again and walked across the room.

Ernest asked, "What does your boyfriend say?"

"Nothing," Hannah told him. "He says nothing useful at all."

"About Iris? Or about everything?"

"Don't change the subject, Ernest," she said.

"Tell me what you want."

"I need to borrow some money," she said, "to take care of her."

I should have seen it coming. With my mother, all roads lead to that. Hannah would tap him for a few thousand, not for a private facility or a hospital or a school, but to get her out of Dodge with her creditors. My mother wouldn't throw good money after something bad like me.

"Well, I've plenty of money," Ernest told her. "You know that."

She smiled. I heard it in her voice.

"And let me have the paintings," she cooed. "I'll take care of them."

"You should have come back before now," he said. "We might have salvaged something."

"You and me?" she said.

"No. Me and Iris."

"You know what your collection means to me," she whispered.

"It means money to you," he said. "I think with Iris it's about the art."

She licked her lips. I heard her.

"Why should I believe a word you say?" Ernest asked her.

"I'm not a monster," Hannah told him. "I am your wife and the mother of your child. Whatever else has passed between us, I am the woman who has given you that."

They were quiet in there for a moment and then Ernest said, "I want to leave Iris something. What can I give her?"

"Just leave her one painting," Hannah said. "Give her that new one. It's not my thing."

"Just one?" he said.

"Leave the rest of them to me," she said. "I wouldn't trust Iris with anything that hasn't already burnt down."

Eighteen

I went down the back stairs to the old kitchen and I cried for exactly one minute, out of anger more than anything. I went through the house like a bug bomb, in and out of everything, picking up anything that could start a fire, cramming it all into my pockets. I emptied Hannah's handbag. I took her lighter and her cigarettes, and her phone too, just to piss her off. Then I came out to get my bike. It was leaning up against the wood store. I tried not to think about that neatly stacked firewood wall splitting and burning and caving in on itself in a heap of fire and rage and ash. I grabbed a stack of old newspapers and a jar of white spirit I found in a shed. I took my bike straight to the other side of the woods, crashed it across long fields and through wet grass and down bone-rattling paths.

I didn't want Ernest hearing that stuff about me. Not from her. I knew what knowing it would do. I thought I could hear it in his voice already – knowledge, contempt and distance. He would wash his hands of me all over again. Who wants to have a problem child? Not him. Not a man who didn't want to be a father in the first place.

I kicked out a big dip in the soft ground with my heels and filled it with dust-dry leaves and snaps of kindling. I struck a match. It made my heartbeat pop like a hit of strong caffeine, like an adrenalin shot. I put the flame to a clutch of dead and tangled grass, dropped it on a nest of papers. It flickered and spread. I crossed cuttings and small branches like a lattice across the top of the bowl, like the bars of a cage, and the fire ate through them, hungry as hell. The air got thick and sharp and my eyes watered. When I dragged some of the larger branches on to the flames and sprinkled them with white spirit, they cracked and sighed and blackened as the thing began to take hold. For a while I stopped thinking. It started to get dark and I was doing a pretty good job of clearing the forest floor of anything fit to burn. It looked like a swept carpet. The fire was huge. They must have heard it booming and crackling from inside the house. They would have seen its vengeful, halo glow, flinging light and shadows out across the fields. I wondered if they watched, or drew the curtains and turned their backs on it. That would be the difference between us.

All night I dragged fallen branches and scrub and clusters of hissing spruce on to the flames. I didn't stop to rest or think. It took up all the air and space and noise in my head. I was trying to burn my mind clean with it.

I explained it to Thurston once, because he was interested, because he bothered to ask. I find it near enough impossible to look anywhere else when there's a fire burning. It dips and flares and travels and breathes, a living thing, and it occupies me completely. I think about how old it is, this scrap of magic, this creator and destroyer, how fundamental and miraculous, how constant and opposite. I think about the dancing, shifting, elusive character of a fire, of the colours it paints, unlike any other colours I will ever find, in a whole lifetime of looking. I am seduced by it. It gets me every time.

Nineteen

In the morning, Hannah came to find me. I heard her moving through the woods before I saw her. I heard the broken cereal crunch of leaves and snapped twigs under her feet. I hadn't slept. My fire was still burning and I was still angry. So was she. The walk through the forest had messed up her hair and ruined her shoes.

"How could you?" I said.

She glared at me, one part mascara, two parts war. "Ernest deserves to hear the truth."

"Why?" I said, and I found it hard to look at her. "What good does it do?"

"That's hardly the point."

I couldn't stand the thought of him lying there in his room, knowing all this about me. I wondered what else

I was supposed to feel, apart from fury and disappointment, apart from shame.

I should have told him myself. She should have let me.

"What was the point of bringing me out here?" I said. "If you were just going to turn him against me, why did I have to come?"

Hannah didn't answer. She just stood there picking bits of leaf and twig off the front of her sweater.

"You ruined everything," I said. "You are such a bitch."

She smiled. "Well there you are, you both probably still agree on something."

I wiped my hands down the sides of my jeans, wiped my face with my sleeve. I was shaking. My fire wasn't working, not any more. I didn't feel calm, or empty, or better. I wanted to scream. I wanted to run. I wanted to hit her. If Thurston had been there he'd have held on to me, and talked me down. He would have understood me, even if nobody else did.

"Anyway," my mother said. "Ernest wants to talk to you."

I asked her what for and she said, "How should I know?"

She stood there with her arms folded, drumming her long fingers on her own elbows. I didn't move.

"Are you coming or aren't you?" she asked me, and I said I didn't know.

"Well, I'm not waiting," she said, brushing her palms together, scratching at her neck, reaching up to fix her hair. "This place is crawling."

"So go," I said. "I didn't ask you to come and get me."

"No," she said. "*He* did."

When she left, I watched her disappearing through the trees and it hit me for the first time just how tired I was of all of it, of being here and being alone and trying to stay upright, trying to be so damn strong. I didn't think I had any fight left in me, so I gave up. I got my bike and followed Hannah back to the house. I couldn't stay by the fire forever, and I had no idea what else I was supposed to do. I didn't catch up and walk with her. I didn't overtake, even though I knew a quicker way. I just stayed behind at a safe distance, like you do when you track a wild animal, because you can never be sure when they are going to turn on you and let down their claws and attack.

I brought the smell of fire into Ernest's room, the proof of my guilt, right there in the air around us. I'd washed my hands and face but my clothes still stank. Hannah went ahead of me up the stairs and when we walked in he didn't take any notice, not at first. Dawn was shaving him without disturbing the oxygen tube that ran between his upper lip and nose like a moustache, keeping his blood fed, given his lungs' reluctance to do so. He didn't say a word until she was finished, and when he did speak, he sounded bone weary. You could hear it.

"Ladies. Leave us, please."

Dawn went first but my mother stayed put with her hands on her hips.

"Are you sure?" she said.

Ernest waved her away with his hand.

"Go and cash your cheque, Hannah," he said. "Go into town and bank it, before I change my mind."

She thought about arguing, I watched her think it through, and then she backed out, closing the door behind her. Ernest motioned for me to open it again so we could be sure she was gone, and not listening like before. Outside, a breeze brushed through the trees. Birds trilled and whistled. Somewhere I could hear a tractor, the odd car passing. Other than that the silence between us felt like lead injected straight into the air. Ernest broke it first.

"Margot was like you," he said. "She felt better when something was burning."

I didn't say anything.

"Cleaner and calmer," he said. "That's what she told me, something like that."

I emptied my pockets on to a table, matches and lighters and rags and sticks and old paper. I said I was sorry he hadn't heard it from me.

"We all have our secrets," he told me. "I wouldn't blame you for that."

I should have said I wouldn't blame him then, for leaving me alone my whole life, but I held it in. I kept it to myself. I still feel bad about that.

"Are you worried now," I asked him. "About your stuff? About your collection and everything, with me here?"

"Should I be?"

I shook my head. "I wouldn't do anything to damage your paintings, or hurt you," I said.

Ernest smiled. "I didn't think so."

"If there's a fire inside this house, I swear it won't be because of me."

"I know," he said. "I believe you."

"I don't know why she told you," I said. "She didn't have to do that."

"*Radix malorum est cupiditas.*"

"What the hell does that mean?"

"The love of money is the root of all evil."

"Yep," I said. "You got that right."

Ernest let out a breath and it hurt him. I could see how much it hurt. I looked around the room. There were three photos of me on the dresser, silver-framed Irises aged one and two and three. I hadn't noticed them before.

"Are you ashamed of me?" I said. "Am I a disappointment?"

"Not at all," he said. "Don't think that."

"I wouldn't blame you," I said. "I really wouldn't."

Ernest shifted himself in the bed. "I could ask you the same thing."

"I used to know how I'd answer," I said. "I don't any more."

"What did Hannah tell you," he said, "about me?"

"Nothing good. Why?"

"I just wondered what you knew."

I looked out of the window because I couldn't look at him.

"She said you weren't cut out to be a father. She said the whole children thing left you cold."

"Not true."

"She said you weren't interested. She said you threw

us out and knew where we were the whole time but you chose never to contact us."

He shook his head. His voice was cracked and swallowed but he got the words out in the end. "She's lying, Iris."

Those pictures you see of people who have spontaneously combusted, those old, black and white photos of a pipe and slippers and just a heap of ash. I was about to be one of those. I could feel it. Any minute now I would be nothing but dust.

Ernest's skin was dull like wax, beaded with sweat. He pressed the button for his morphine, three times. He looked up at the ceiling. His eyes kept closing. He dropped off for about twenty seconds and then his breathing stopped and he woke right back up again with a start, like something made him jump.

"It was impossible," he said. "So I gave up."

"What was impossible? Being my dad?"

"All the questions I asked," he said, "and the people I paid, who tried and failed."

"What do you mean," I asked him, "*people you paid?* What are you talking about?"

"I would have traced them there," he told me, words slurring slightly, "but they changed their names."

"Ernest," I told him. "Look at me. I'm Iris, right? I'm not Margot. Do you know that?"

He looked at me sideways. He didn't turn his head.

"Funny," he said. "If Lowell had found any kind of success as an actor, I'd have found you."

"Were you looking for me?" I said, and I felt this thundering in my chest, like horses' hooves, like the spilling lip of a waterfall. "I didn't know you were looking for me."

Ernest closed his eyes again. He spoke without opening them. "For over twelve years. One hundred and forty-six months. Six hundred and thirty-two weeks."

I moved closer to him, dragging the old smell of burning halfway across his room.

"Four thousand, four hundred and twenty-six days, to be precise," he said.

"You counted?" I asked him, and something bloomed in my head when I said it, something like wonder, or relief.

He nodded. "Where did they get the name 'Baxter' from anyway," he said, like I would know. "A tin of soup?"

"What are you saying?" I asked. "They changed their names? Why would they do that?"

Ernest was quiet for a moment. I think he was deciding

on the right words. High up in my chest I felt the buzz and flap of wings, like a flock of birds, or those hillsides thick with butterflies, or a swarm of bees.

"So I wouldn't find them," he said. "So I wouldn't find you."

"But they didn't want me," I said. "Not really."

"No, but I did."

I think I steadied myself at the foot of his bed. I think I looked down at my fingers clinging on there. I remember I felt like I wasn't in the room, not any more, and also that I'd never been more in a room in my life.

"You weren't the only thing they stole from me," Ernest said, and he turned his face to the window, "but you were the most precious."

I sat down. I saw the shape of his legs in the bed, thin and wasted, and I sat beside him.

"And if they did this to you," I said.

"To us," he interrupted.

"Then why would they come here? Why would they bring me back?"

He shrugged. "I've asked myself the same question. I think they ran out of rope."

"And you were ill," I said.

"A real gift horse," Ernest added. "A real piece of luck, for them."

He was paler than ever, contorted somehow against the pain.

"Call the nurse," he said. "I'm sorry. This is unbearable."

I went out into the hallway and shouted for her. She wasn't far. I heard her running. When I came back, Ernest reached for my hand and I held on to it.

"Stay, please," he said. "Don't leave before me."

I could feel his panic like static through the tips of his fingers. I'm surprised my heart didn't swell and burst free of my chest at that, his fear, his brave smile when our eyes met. I'm surprised Dawn didn't have to get down and defibrillate it, where it landed at her feet.

Ernest and I could have been Father and Daughter. We could have been such good friends.

Dawn was calm and she knew what to do – an intravenous dose of something, a jab of something else. Ernest's face softened and his grip on my hand did too.

"How's the pain, Ernest?" she asked.

His eyes were shut. "Magnificent."

"Still got your sense of humour I see."

"Hanging on by a thread," Ernest told her. "Hanging on by a thread."

He pulled at my hand until I got closer and bent down to hear him speak.

"Your mother will be back soon," he whispered. "There isn't much time."

"I'm listening, Ernest," I said. "I'm here."

Twenty

Ernest painted my mother a few times at the beginning, never successfully. Apparently, Hannah was a terrible life model. She couldn't sit still. She couldn't seem to hold a thought in her head long enough for him to get it on to the canvas. Even his sketches of her lacked something. He said, "It was like trying to see into a woman made of chrome."

He thought it was his mistake but later he saw that those sketches were pretty accurate, and that what he was getting was a clear picture of who she was now, all surface, all restlessness and emptiness and boredom. She'd erased her past until there was nothing left.

Hannah filled the house with people. She said if they weren't allowed to live in London, then London would have to come to them. She never tired of flaunting her new money before her friends. Lowell Baxter was a regular fixture apparently, dark and striking, the planes and lines of his face so accurate, so perfect that he seemed to be made of something different to the rest of them, he and Hannah both.

"Of course," he told me, "that wasn't his name then. When I knew him, his name was William Lowe."

"That's who you searched for?"

"It's why I didn't find you."

Ernest couldn't stand Lowell, from the first moment. He said he oozed into the house like floodwater, coating everything in the same dark matter, cutting off its air supply. Hannah said he was just jealous.

"He's harmless," my mother told him. "It's me you should be worried about."

Most mornings, while Hannah slept, Ernest went to work in his studio, a converted grain store behind the house. It was invisible, just like he was. I've been in it a hundred times now. You'd never guess it was there, if you didn't know. From the outside it's just a wind-ravaged, tumbledown outbuilding. Inside, you step down into a white, paint-splattered cube with enough glass in its ramshackle roof to flood the place with natural light. My mother didn't set foot in there, not once. She didn't notice when he went to meet dealers in London or Paris or Amsterdam or New York. She never wondered where Ernest was when he was gone. She wasn't interested in what he was doing or when he might be coming back. She just enjoyed the time without him.

He said, "For our first anniversary I bought her a Chagall painting."

Thurston told me a story about Marc Chagall. He asked a group of children looking at one of his stained-glass pieces in the cathedral at Reims, "Do you understand Chagall?" and they said, "Yes, we do."

"That's strange," the artist told them, "because I don't understand him at all."

"Which one?" I asked Ernest. "Is it *The Promenade*? I think I've seen it downstairs."

Green prism hills and houses, a pastel pink church, a red crumpled picnic blanket and a man, trapping a bird with one hand, and holding on to his weightless, floating lover with the other. Ernest said it was meant to be a celebration of Chagall's blissful marriage to Bella Rosenfeld. But when Ernest saw it, he could only think the man was anchoring her there to stop her from getting away.

My mother left him seven times. Sometimes he only knew where she was because of the credit card bills –

restaurants in Nice and Copenhagen, spas in Morzine and Milan, department stores in London and New York. It got a little easier when she left, each time. He hardly survived the first. The second and third, he couldn't eat, or think, or breathe. But he could work. When Hannah was away, he said that was all he did.

"Dealing art?" I asked.

"I made money," he nodded, "and I stored it like a dam against the possibility of her leaving me for good. She always came back to the money, like an ant to sugar."

They lived like that for more than five years. And then one morning Hannah came into the kitchen and stood across from him at the table. Ernest was just getting up. She was on her way to bed. She turned to look out at the garden and he remembered the first time she had stood there, and all the fine things he had hoped for them, at the beginning.

"I'm pregnant," she said, and with a sharp laugh added, "God knows how."

Ernest put his cup down, got up and walked to where she was standing. He put his arms around her and Hannah burst into tears.

"She cried?" I said. "My mother cried?" I'd never seen her do that.

She cried while he put her to bed. She cried while he told her friends it was over now, and time to go home. She cried while he cooked and cleaned, while he painted and repainted the nursery. She cried because the party was over, because he'd trapped her, and wouldn't let her drink. She cried because she felt like a whale, and couldn't sleep, and had to pee every five minutes. Ernest put up with her whining and wallowing because finally it wasn't all for nothing. He put up with it for their coming child, for me, I suppose, because at last, he said, he was dealing with something that was perfectly real.

Fibonacci's Golden Ratio is the mathematical principle of beauty, 1:1.62. Leonardo da Vinci called it the divine proportion, like God had a tape measure or something. A perfect face is 1.62 times longer than it is wide. A body should be 1.62 times longer from the belly button to the feet than from the same spot to the top of the head. A nose ought to be 1.62 times narrower, at its widest point, than a mouth. It's simple. Everything in art and architecture and nature obeys the same rule. If a thing doesn't measure up, it's not beautiful and that isn't a matter of opinion, it is a mathematical fact. Thurston told me I should always remember that Mr Fibonacci came up with his golden ratio, his perfect number in nature, while he was watching rabbits screwing. He said it was the best reason he knew to be less judgemental about how other people spent their time.

According to Fibonacci, I'm not beautiful. No big surprise. None of my numbers are right, and that's fine by me. But according to Ernest, I was better than da Vinci's *The Last Supper*, or Michelangelo's *The Creation of Adam*, or Botticelli's *The Birth of Venus*, or George Seurat's *Bathers at Asnières* or Burne-Jones's *The Golden Stairs*, all flawless examples of the divine proportion in action. Bullshit, obviously, the final ramblings of a fond and dying man, but Ernest persisted.

He said, "You were the first time I had ever, in my life, preferred real life to art."

I was born three weeks early, by Caesarean section, and I don't think my mother will ever forgive me for those scars. Afterwards, she slept and Ernest stayed up, watching me in my plastic, fish-tank crib. There were wires attached to my chest. He said I jerked and shuddered in my sleep, as if all of my dreams were about falling, and my hands opened and closed like tiny stars. He said I was no bigger than a bird.

We were in the hospital for a week. The midwives

talked only to Hannah, as if Ernest was just there to carry the bags, but he listened because he knew it would be him taking care of me. He knew Hannah wasn't interested, not really. She might try, but something as demanding as a child would fail to hold her interest for long.

The first time she handed me to Ernest she said, "Sorry it's not a boy. I imagine you'd have preferred that."

It was a warm, dry summer. Ernest fed and bathed and dressed me. He read in the garden and I kicked at my blankets in the shade of the old sycamore tree. He sang me to sleep, all the songs and rhymes he remembered from his own childhood. He stopped work. When I was born, Ernest lost interest in money.

He said, "Your mother found that very hard to comprehend."

For nearly four years, he took care of me while she took up her life where she'd left off. The house filled with people again, and Hannah's trips away grew longer and closer together. Ernest stayed behind. He says he was with me when I saw my first moon, my first horse, my first bird's egg and my first puddle. Ernest was with me, not Hannah. It was him I went to if I fell and hurt my knees. It was him I looked for with a fever or a question or a gift.

I wished more than anything that I could remember it. I said so, and Ernest looked sadder than I'd ever seen him, and nodded.

"So do I," he said. "So do I."

The day after Hannah's thirtieth birthday, the weekend crowd had thinned and straggled home, but Lowell's car squatted low on the drive, coiled and mean-looking, like something about to pounce. Hannah came round the side of the house. She hadn't meant to bump into Ernest. He said he could tell by the look on her face.

He asked her where she was going.

"I'm leaving you," she said. "I'm not coming back."

I was in the back of Lowell's car. Ernest could see me. I was playing with my bear. I must have been four.

"I've tried," she said, "because you're so dependable and so rich. And you're a good babysitter, Ernest, you always have been. But I can't do it any more. I can't stand you."

"William appeared to have money back then," he told me, and I had to remember who he was talking about, remember that William was Lowell. "Hannah must have thought it would last longer than it did."

He said she would never have left him if she'd known that everything was on credit, all borrowed against

Lowell's ambition, the power of his positive thinking and astronomical self-belief.

"How do you know all that?" I said.

"I had him investigated. William Lowe. Bankrupt, defaulted, then gone. He vanished, owing thousands. I always thought your mother would come back to me when she found that out."

"And you'd have let her?"

"I'd have done anything, Iris, to see you."

"You can't just take our daughter," he told her. "It's illegal. I can stop you from doing that."

Hannah looked like she almost felt sorry for him and then the steel shutters came down behind her eyes.

"Just watch me," she said.

Twenty-one

Whenever I think about a fire, I trace it back to its very beginning, when it's still nothing, when it hasn't even happened yet. An un-struck match, an unwanted cigarette end, each humble thing on the edge of greatness, each thing giddy with potential. I think about fires in forests and cities and hillsides. I visited the monument to the Great Fire of London when we flew back, tall and straight as a candle, its height the exact distance it stands from the spark that started the fire. I climbed the 311 steps to the viewing platform. I watched a film of the same view, a time-lapse video of the city, where the lights flicker on and off like blown embers and the cranes wave like insects' legs at the passing sky.

I thought about the tiny seed of hatred Hannah planted in me the first time she told me about my real father, the little sparks of rage she fanned when she said he didn't want me, wasn't interested, hadn't cared.

And I'd been thinking the same way about Thurston, trying to isolate the moment things started falling apart, the misplaced card that caused all the other cards to fall. I couldn't help what my mother had done, but Thurston was my fault. I'm as certain as I could be of that.

Thurston made something for me. That's all he did. He asked me to meet him and he said I should bring a candle.

"But no petrol," he said. "This isn't bonfire night."

"Well, what is it then?"

"It's a gift," he said. "You've got to see it. It's all for you."

The address he gave me was downtown, near the church on Hill Street that looks like a club. Thurston wasn't there, but at the corner I could see the flickering lights of other candles spread out on the sidewalk, so I went that way. There were a few people there, come out of the church mostly, I could tell from the loud slogans on their T-shirts, SO LOVED and GET YOUR BRAVE ON. I could tell from their too-good-to-be-true smiles. It was a shrine to someone. I kept walking, and when I got right up to the middle of it, I saw it was a shrine to me.

Thurston had tied flowers to the railings and left notes and pictures as well as candles. I could see almost all of them were his, more than ten photos and drawings of me, different sizes, some covered with plastic, some faded and softened already by the heat of the sun and the damp, humid nights. It must have been there for a few days. People had started to add their own best wishes and souvenirs. I watched someone leave a single rose. I saw a woman and her daughter stop to look, and frown at each other with their hands on their hearts, and move on. Somebody lit my candle and I put it on the ground with all the others. I read a few of the messages, SUFFER LITTLE CHILDREN TO COME UNTO ME, AND FORBID THEM NOT. LIGHT A FIRE IN HEAVEN IRIS B. GONE BUT NOT FORGOTTEN XXX. He'd drawn my eye too, right there on the tarmac – the sharp black pupil, the clean white ball, the swirling bright circle of colour.

"Shit," I said, under my breath, and I was thinking that this pretend, dead Iris had more friends than me. I was thinking that if I really died, nobody would leave notes like that, or flowers. There would be no drawings or photos or soft toys. I was almost jealous of her. It made me more sad than anything else. It was a lousy present.

I stood up and looked around for Thurston because he'd be there somewhere on the edge of it, enjoying himself, watching the thing he'd made become more than the sum of its parts. I should have kept my head down because that's when someone recognised me. A girl about my age with tight, pulled-back hair and wide black eyes, dilated like hollows, pointed at me and her mouth kind of fell open and I suddenly knew this was what Thurston had been hoping for all along. I was the girl who showed up at her own shrine. I was Lazarus. Somebody reached out and touched me. Someone else took my picture. The news passed between them like a current, like electricity. They didn't take their eyes off me and they talked to one another like I couldn't hear them, like I wasn't really there. "Is that her?" "Did she say something?" "Does she have a message?" "What's going on?"

One of them made the sign of the cross. Some guy dropped to his knees right there in front of me.

"It's not real," I said. "It's a joke. It's just a bad joke," and I tried to back away, but they were behind me too, stopping me, and there were more of them than before. I was stuck. I was surrounded.

I felt Thurston before I saw him. He came up behind

me, flipped something over my head and walked me out of there and out of sight, double-quick. They shouted at us. A few of them followed. We hid in a doorway down the block.

The hood was still over my head and Thurston shielded me from the street, his chest pressed up against my back. I was on the very edge of something, right there in that doorway, I could see it was about to happen, but instead I just got angry, because angry was way easier to do. I rammed my elbow hard into his ribs.

"What the hell was that for?" he said, stepping back fast. It shocked him, my fury. I don't think he'd seen it before.

"Screw you," I said.

"You didn't like it?"

"No, I hated it."

"People have been paying their respects for days," he said.

"That's your gift to me, is it?" I asked him.

He said I was the miracle those people could take home and give thanks for before supper. He said, "You are their proof of the existence of God."

"Are you mocking me?" I said. "Don't do that, Thurston. Don't you do that."

"Don't you get it, Iris? I thought you'd get it."

He was right. I did. It was classic Thurston and I should have rolled with it and played along. But for some reason I'd decided to fight him, and even though half of me wanted to, I couldn't seem to back down.

"You think people don't see you," he said. "You think you're forgettable. But those people saw you. They won't forget."

"I don't want people to see me," I said. "Not like that."

"Sure you do. You're always saying stuff about it."

"Don't make me the butt of one of your jokes ever again," I told him. "Not without asking."

"Iris," he said. "What is this?"

I didn't say anything.

"Aren't we best friends?" he said. "Better than that?"

"I don't know," I told him. "I don't know what we are."

"What does that even mean?"

I shrugged.

"What do you want from me, Thurston?" I said. "Do you want me to be grateful?"

He shook his head. "How come you can't see how much you're loved?"

I couldn't look at him. I thought to myself, when

someone puts you high up like that, in the end it's just further to fall.

"Just leave me alone," I said.

"IRIS," Thurston said. "What are you talking about?"

"I don't think we should see each other for a while," I said, and I've no idea why. I didn't mean it. I guess I was trying to break something before it got broken, which is stupid, and for what it's worth I've been paying for it ever since.

"Are you serious?" Thurston said.

"Yes, I'm serious," I lied. "Why wouldn't I be?"

"I'm SORRY," he said. "I told you I'm sorry."

"Not good enough," I said.

"If you break this," he said. "I swear to God, I'll—"

"You'll what, Thurston? You'll fucking what?"

And because I was angry with him, I walked away before he could tell me.

I shouldn't have said what I said. I should have laughed, and taken his hand and gone with him to the beach or the hills or wherever he asked me to go. But those were the last words I said to Thurston. It was the last time I saw him before we left.

That week I looked for him in all the usual places but he wasn't there. Not by the bread shop on Monday, not in Griffith Park on Tuesday, or at my apartment block on Wednesday and Thursday, or outside school on Friday morning with a plan, like always. He stayed away because I told him to but really it was the last thing I wanted.

Friday afternoon in class, I was going crazy. I guess I'd had enough. I stole a key to one of the upstairs store cupboards. I walked through the halls, quiet and empty apart from my footsteps because everyone was in class. The store cupboard was just a room, shelved from floor to ceiling, quiet and dark and dusty, stacked with textbooks and art paper and old costumes and equipment. The door was heavy and it swung shut quick behind me and I should have checked that I could open it again but I didn't. I was in too much of a hurry. I didn't even look for the light switch. I just leaned against the wall in the dark.

The matchbook was in my pocket, tight against my hip. Flat, blue-black, glossy, it fitted neatly in the palm of my hand. The matches were planted in two tight rows, one behind the other, lined up together underneath the cover, white with black tips. Lowell had left it in his coat. It had someone's phone number scrawled on it, someone's lipstick mark, not Hannah's. One match was torn off. A scar ran across the base where it had been struck. There were thirteen left.

I lit one and put it to the corners of some old posters stuck up behind me on the wall. I dropped one into a nest of old papers. I tore the pages out of some books on a shelf top, crumpled them in my fists and set them alight as well. Everything was dried out and happy to burn. The only light in the room came from the flames.

I set fires in all four corners of the room and stood in the middle watching them lick and snap and spread together. Shadows reared up against the walls. The shelves caught fire, and then the stacked tables and the frame of the door. The heat began to bend itself tightly around me, and things began to break and flare and pop. I heard the rumble in the air the fire made, like faraway thunder, like a herd of distant cattle and then the air began to spit and hum and crackle. I tried the door handle but it wouldn't move. I did it again but the lock was stuck shut. I couldn't get it open. My hair started to shrink and sizzle in the heat. I could taste fire in my mouth. My eyes were scorched and dry and my lungs were already heaving with the smoke.

Nobody heard me banging on the door, not to start with. I think I was coughing, bent double on the floor in the raging dark when they broke it down. I think they smashed the lock with an axe. The fire leapt out into the hallway like a caged lion. I heard them all as if I was underwater. I saw them from behind glass. The blood moved through my veins like molasses, everything slowed down and sticky. My throat burned raw and my chest felt weighted down with concrete, wrapped in iron.

The alarm was wailing and I realised it had been wailing for some time before it reached me. The janitor and a couple of teachers swooped in with their eyes rolling in their heads and the fire extinguishers spoiling everything with white foam. When they saw me they started yelling and one of them dragged me out into the hallway and covered me with a coat, or a blanket. One of them stayed with me. He didn't touch me but I could hear his voice and he was telling me over and over that things were going to be OK, as if he knew.

By the time the fire truck and the ambulance arrived, the whole building had been evacuated. The place was bitter with damp smoke. Foam and ash mixed together like sludge. Everyone walked in it on their way out, spreading it about, like a blanket of snow fallen pure and spotless overnight until the people come out and spoil the morning, turning everything used and dirty-grey.

I lay very still and pictured Thurston's shrine, the notes and photos, the drawings and flowers. I thought if I died now, if this fire killed me, then he'd think I was punishing him. Thurston would think that of me, even if it wasn't true.

"All for you," he had said, and I was shocked at myself, at the way I'd reacted, and at what I'd just almost done.

At the hospital, I had to wait for someone to come and claim me. The same teacher who found me stayed in my room like a prison guard. Mr Banks, from the biology department. Everything about him was the colour of cement, his shirt and slacks and tank top, his shoes and hair and skin. He looked just like a statue propped there against the wall, so I pretended he was one, and ignored him.

I got a psychiatric interview. Actually I got three. The nurse then the doctors then a social worker asked me the same prying, obvious questions about my levels of happiness and any trouble at home. They asked me if I had meant to hurt myself, or hurt others. I said no to both. I said it was a stupid accident. I said I wasn't a self-harmer, nothing like that, and they looked at me like they'd heard it all before, which they probably had, but not from me. They dressed my burns and filled me with fluids and antibiotics. They treated my scalded lungs with pure oxygen and raised their eyebrows meaningfully at each other over my head. I didn't want to speak to any of them. I didn't want to answer anyone's questions.

They couldn't get hold of Hannah or Lowell. Big surprise. Both of their phones were switched off. I was in no fit state to leave, they said, not until they were satisfied with my progress, and definitely not without a parent or guardian. I wanted to see Thurston then more than I'd ever wanted anything before. I wanted to say thank you and sorry and please, please help me get the hell out of here. My clothes were gone. My lungs were the size of teabags. I couldn't have escaped if I'd tried. I heard them talk about hospitalising me. They discussed hypoxia and presentation of symptoms and lack of co-operation. A fly was trying to find its way out through a window. It was drilling a hole through the glass with its wings. It wouldn't give up. There was a fly like that inside my body. I could feel it drilling in my skull.

When my mother finally arrived, she was sweating under her make-up, all the careful layers of basecoat and highlight and concealer starting to slip. I could smell the vodka on her breath at ten paces. She was in the mood for a fight and I worried she'd had just enough alcohol to start one and just too much to be able to win it. I picked at the bandages on my hands and kept my mouth and my eyes tight shut. I pretended none of this was happening, not to anyone I knew and definitely not to me.

She stood outside in the hallway with Mr Banks and lied at the top of her voice. He was trying to say something sensitive and understanding, he wanted to demonstrate the school's concern, but my mother wasn't buying into that. Never own up if you can help it. That was the Baxter way. Every time he opened his mouth to speak, she cut him off.

She said, "There is no way this fire was started by my daughter."

She said the school was negligent. She said there must have been something dangerous in the storeroom for it to burst into flames like that with a child inside it.

She said, "Have you got CCTV in that cupboard? No? Well good luck proving it."

She said, "You are very lucky something worse didn't happen to her on school property. You should be grateful nobody else got hurt. You should be grateful *we* are not suing *you*."

The social worker and one of the doctors took Hannah into another room down the hall. I could still hear her voice, raised high above the others. I wondered how long my mother would pay attention before she decided she needed a cigarette, or another drink, or just to get the hell out of there because everyone was so serious and ordinary and ugly and she didn't belong. She hated being made to feel like the responsible adult. They asked her if she'd brought me any fresh clothes. She looked at them like they were the ones not taking this seriously.

"I. Was. At. Lunch," she said.

I stayed the night. The next day, when Hannah reappeared, without my clothes, they gave me a hospital T-shirt and sweatpants and let me leave as an outpatient. I had strict instructions for the next twenty four hours, a follow-up appointment to check on my burns. Hannah signed all the necessary forms and paid with a cheque that wouldn't cash. I saw her write down the wrong address and phone number. There wasn't any money in the kitty for medical bills. We wouldn't be coming back.

I'd heard them arguing about money the night before I did it. They owed nearly twenty grand in bills and back rent. Their credit cards were maxed out. Hannah was drunk and online, trying to book plane tickets back to the UK. Lowell didn't want to go.

"What choice do we have?" she hissed at him. "We came out here so you could make it, and you plainly haven't."

Lowell groaned. "It's your nut-job daughter's fault I didn't get that mini-series," he said. "Who lit a fire upstairs when the casting director was here? I had that role in the bag before she assaulted his kid."

Hannah carried on typing. "Well my nut-job daughter is going to need medical help at this rate, thousands of dollars' worth. She's a lawsuit waiting to happen. Let's get her back to the NHS, shall we? Let's get her back to her bastard millionaire father, and tap him for some cash."

"She's ruined everything," Lowell told her, "your stupid kid."

Hannah sloshed more vodka into their glasses. "Believe me, I've thought about that more often than you have. It's time to get out before she burns down a mall and everyone knows our business. Drink to it, Lowell. Give it up. It's time to go."

When we got outside the hospital, I looked for Thurston on the street, even though I knew he wouldn't be there. Everybody was him, for half a second, until they weren't. My mother stopped and lit a cigarette. Her hair was coming loose and a strand of it was stuck to the hot skin of her neck. She looked up and then down Sunset Boulevard, getting her bearings, and then we set off heading west and turned right, towards Barnsdall Park. Hannah was tall as a giraffe in her Louboutins. A big woman walked past us on the other side of the street, tipping from side to side as she moved. Her ankles were as plump and swollen as the tops of her arms.

"That is the only time I do that for you," Hannah said, looking again and again at the fat woman, like there was too much of her to see in one go. "Next time you're on your own."

"Can we take a cab?" I asked. "I feel kind of light-headed."

"No money for cabs," Hannah said. "I used my last twenty getting here." She showed me her empty wallet and pulled a sad face. "The cupboard is bare. You can rest when we get home. You can go to bed and you can damn well stay there."

We walked down Vermont and turned left on Hollywood. I felt weak and hollow and dizzy. I thought my lungs were going to break out of my chest. In the park, I watched a little boy running wide, joyful circles around his dad. I saw a family lying back on a picnic rug. Somebody tall and skinny walked towards us on the path and I willed it to be Thurston, come to rescue me, but of course it wasn't, he didn't. The boy was tall and skinny but he was a disappointment, a total stranger, and he walked straight by.

"So," Hannah said, not looking at me. "I know you started that fire. The question is, did you admit it?"

A breeze moved in the leaves around us. I could see it passing. I could see where it went.

"No," I said. "But they probably know."

"For God's sake," she yelled at me. A couple of people looked over.

"What," I said, "did I ruin everything?"

"Is there anything we failed to give you?" Hannah asked. "Do you lack for anything, anything at all?" and because I didn't know how to even begin answering that question, I didn't try.

"You'll end up in a madhouse, or a prison. Arson is a very serious offence."

"They're called psychiatric hospitals," I told her. "You don't say madhouse. You don't say madhouse and you don't say nut-job."

Hannah turned on me, jabbing her pointed finger against the flat, sore bones of my chest. "You do not get to tell me what I do and don't say, young lady. Not now and not ever."

"You're bothered about paying for it, aren't you," I said, "if I get in trouble. If I get locked up, or sectioned," and Hannah slapped me then, across the cheek, which I took as a yes.

We walked in silence for a minute and then she said, "You've burned our bridges. That's what you've done."

Nice pun, I thought, please God tell me she's not going to ask me what people would say.

"What would people say?" She stopped abruptly on the narrow path, flinging her hands towards the trees.

"It won't happen again," I lied. "I won't get caught again," I said, which was the truth.

Twenty-two

Ernest said the consultant who passed on his death sentence was young and exact and carefully sympathetic. He pinched his suit trousers straight before he sat down.

"Nice socks," Ernest told him after the bad news, after he'd taken it in and found that he was still breathing. The socks were pink with red spots. Ernest said you couldn't miss them.

The consultant looked lost for a second, like an actor asked to come out of character, and then he smiled and said, "Thanks. My daughter gave them to me."

Ernest felt the word 'daughter' like a blade in his side. He said he'd had a daughter once and then lost her.

"I'm so sorry," the doctor told him. "Did she die?"

Ernest was getting ready to leave the room. He'd already put on his jacket.

"Honestly?" he said. "I've no idea."

All the way home he said he thought harder than ever about where I might be at that precise moment, what I might be doing, living or dead. He thought about his doctor, charged with the task of telling him that after all the chemo and radio and surgery, there was nothing more to be done. He thought about what he might say to the next patient, and the one after that, in life-changing fifteen-minute slots, all day long, until he could go home and put his pink and red polka-dot feet up, and be with his daughter, and try to forget.

He said, "I thought about everything but the facts in front of me, because I didn't want to think about those."

Even while the doctor was explaining it all, a large part of Ernest decided he was wrong. It was the only way to put one foot in front of the other, the only way he could stay upright and get through the waiting room, out into the car park, round the one-way system and home. I suppose his brain was hardwired to ignore the truth so it could get on until the very last second with the business of living.

But what if death is the one and only way that you do get to live forever? If the weight of the universe never changes, regardless of who's living and who's dying, that must mean we never leave it, not entirely. If I become a scrap of smoke and dust, if Ernest's ashes get flung high into the wind from his top windows, if Thurston's body falls to the bottom of the sea, if Lowell's is picked apart by birds and Hannah's is buried and melts slowly back to soil, aren't we all still somewhere? Aren't we all still here?

Death might be the one true fact, the one thing you can rely on, but nobody wants to hear about it. You start trying to put a positive spin on the whole idea and you can clear the room quicker than a bad DJ at a wedding. Death is off limits. That's why we put a hood on the executioner. None of us wants to see his face.

I told Ernest that if I could, I'd come from the planet Tralfamadore, where time is like a stretch of the Rocky Mountains, and moments are like clusters of beads on a string, laid out before you, all there at once. There is no cause and effect, no before or then or next or after. There is no difference between what was, or is, or will be. You can exist and not exist on the same string, at the same time.

"You can be dead and still alive," I said, "if you're a Tralfamadorian."

Ernest laughed and the world's oceans gathered in his chest and tried to drown him. "Who said that? When can we travel?"

"It's Kurt Vonnegut," I said. "He died already. If there's such a thing as the afterlife, you'll have to look for him when you get there."

I told him when Kurt Vonnegut fell down the stairs at his home at the age of 84, one newspaper wrote that reports of his death shouldn't be believed without checking Dresden for his younger self first.

Ernest had never read any Kurt Vonnegut. I pitied him and envied him all at once, that he'd missed out and that he had it still to come. I told him that Vonnegut was a Prisoner of War in Dresden and a witness to the Allied bombings in 1945. He came up from underground and almost everyone was dead, almost everything burnt to the ground. He was twenty-two years old. He had a lot to make sense of, and after more than twenty years of trying not to think about it, he wrote Slaughterhouse Five, and invented Tralfamadore.

Thurston read that whole book to me out loud. He lay with his head in my lap and the book between him and the sun. It took about a week. I might never have been happier.

"I'll read it to you," I told Ernest, "if we have time." We didn't.

I tried to see Ernest's life as a string of beads. I looked

at pictures of him as a young man, balancing on a fencepost, leaning against a wall, squinting into the sun. I found a photo of their wedding day, he and my mother on the steps of the registry office, and below them a woman pushing a pram, a blur of cyclist, and a man out walking his dog.

"Why did you never divorce?" I asked him.

"I'd need her signature. I couldn't find her."

"But if someone disappears for that long," I said, "surely—"

"She's still my wife," he said. "My next of kin."

He looked again at the wedding picture.

"I can't still be there now," he said, "because everything is different."

Ernest was right. This isn't the planet Tralfamadore, or anything like it. Everything here is bound by beginning and end, apart from the Universe, which is not only infinite but also expanding. I have a problem with something infinite getting any bigger, and I had a problem with Ernest's death. I needed a stop sign, a pause button. Not quite, not now, not yet.

Ernest said I shouldn't worry. He said he was close enough to see it quite clearly, and given that he couldn't stop it if he tried, he might as well admit, it wasn't such a long way down.

Twenty-three

The world doesn't end when the world ends, by the way; it keeps right on turning. The world ends and you get up and put your clothes on and clean your teeth and eat your breakfast like nothing has changed at all. It made me sick to my stomach after Ernest died, that I still found things funny, that I still got hungry or tired or bored or distracted, that after a while I started to forget about him for whole minutes and hours and days at a time. It made me want to burn something down, that I'd spent so many years acting like he didn't exist when he was right there all the time. I didn't think I could ever forgive my mother for what she did. I could set fire to every last thing in the world she possessed and it wouldn't begin to change how I felt about that.

Ernest's last few days were strange and slow and

fragile. We were very careful with each other. Every single thing we said and did seemed to have weight, seemed important. We were learning to live with it, I suppose, with what we knew for sure was about to happen. We were separate, like islands. He was separate, anyway. I think that's the point I'm trying to make. Part of him had already sailed.

He and my mother must have come to some kind of arrangement because three days before he died she suddenly backed off. She lost interest in the whole thing and went away. She took the Bentley. I figured she left because dying is so unglamorous and wretched and contagious and she didn't want to have any part in it. Whatever. It gave us some space at least, my father and me. It gave us some time alone together at the end. Lowell phoned once or twice while she was still here, but only to talk about how good the catering was on set and how humble and down-to-earth the other actors were, like they were from another galaxy or something. He never called to engage with what was actually happening, in the real world, to us.

On his last whole day, we carried Ernest downstairs, the nurses and me, and laid him in the garden, with cushions and blankets and oxygen and the sun on his face. He watched me and I knew what he was doing.

I slipped my arm through his and said, "Stop it," but he'd already done it. It was too late. He'd been doing it for days now, picturing the world without him in it. He was erasing himself from his usual place, withdrawing, saying goodbye, because it seemed like the right thing to do.

Ernest said it was a bit like being in love with someone who doesn't love you back. The very fact that they don't need you makes them a thousand times more desirable and beautiful and the object of your devotion. Sometimes it's the impossibility of a thing that makes it irresistible. And right then, being alive was the thing he was in love with, the thing that didn't care if he was there or not. Every leaf, every blade of grass, every bug and footprint and pebble was bathed in a new kind of light for him. I knew I couldn't see it the way he could. Every single thing Ernest looked at was breathtakingly, effortlessly, perfectly itself. Even the most ordinary thing he could think of – a dustbin, a lamppost, an envelope – was part of the biggest, most persuasive, most extraordinary miracle there is, as solid as a rock and at the same time as fine and breakable as a single hair.

He said, "When you know for certain you are losing a thing, you suddenly see how much you have loved it, and how you ought to have taken better care of it all along."

It was dark when he died. Outside, bands of mist dropped on to the garden, obscuring everything, and then were just as suddenly gone. I sat with him, with Jane and Lisa and Dawn, me with my feet and my knees pressed together, my hands in my lap, my face composed, because I had no say in anything else but my own reaction. I tried to hold him with me in the room, to keep him here, but I couldn't do it. There was a storm coming and the trees thrashed in the wind. The air bellowed and cracked and the rain began to lash against his windows, louder and louder, until there was a noise above me like a filling sail, like a parachute opening. I pretended it was the sound of angels landing. I pictured a legion of them on the roof, their wings cumbersome and wide, punching great holes in the air. I thought maybe they had come for him. He was ready to go. I figured that's what happens when you get that close. It's just a step down, no big deal. I hoped so anyway. I hoped he was watching us by then from another place entirely, somewhere quiet and painless and apart. And while I was hoping, and holding his hand, he slipped away.

They left me alone with him. For a while he was still warm, and I convinced myself that he wasn't all gone, that part of him still occupied the high corners of the room. I stroked his hand, slack and heavy now, his emptied skin like a breeze on the surface of still water. I'm sure I spoke to him but I don't remember what I said. Ernest's face was the same and not the same, a quiet house, his lips bloodless and tight as if stitched to his teeth, his flesh deflated like punctured dough, sunk and settled closer to its bones. It shocked me how quickly he abandoned it. Just so you know, dead doesn't look like sleeping. Dead looks gone.

Some of his things were on the bedside table. His watch, his toothbrush, a comb, everyday objects that seemed instantly, overwhelmingly significant because they were his, or had been, and useless too, because he wouldn't need them, not again. There was a book and a half-finished crossword, and I knew already that I'd start reading it, that I'd solve the last few clues in an effort to inch nearer to him now that he was so finally and irretrievably lost. Pointless, I knew, too late, but I'd do it anyway.

Dawn came back in with her head bowed and her hands clasped. I heard her voice from very far away. I was a wasp in a jar and she was talking to me. She told me that Ernest didn't suffer, that he wasn't in any pain.

"He knew what was coming," she said, "and he wasn't alone. You were with him and he wasn't afraid."

I was grateful. I wondered if she said that to everyone. I wanted very much for some of it to be true.

Later, when I couldn't sleep, I found myself looking for him everywhere, waiting for him to come back. I didn't find him in the drawers of mildewed papers I emptied, in the pockets of his dun-coloured overcoat, English made, the same as his dad's. He wasn't smiling from the countless drawings of faces at crowded tables, of long-ago parties and marble statues and elegant cities, all the sketches that he asked me to clear out and round up and burn. He wasn't in the half-drunk bottle of milk in his fridge. I saw it and it felt like an insult, like a punch in the stomach, that the milk was still fresh and Ernest was gone forever.

I looked at more old pictures – a freckled boy with strong cheekbones and straight teeth and an undiluted light in his eyes. I hadn't seen them before. I was sure I'd looked in that photo album and found nothing. One last check and there he was, smiling right at me from forty years ago. It felt like an extra moment of his life, an instant's grace. I figured then that as long as I could keep finding new things about him, Ernest wouldn't be completely dead.

Twenty-four

The night before Ernest's funeral, I dreamt about Thurston. He was standing so close to me that I could smell the exact warm smell of his skin, even in my sleep. He didn't say a word in my dream but when I woke up I had the definite feeling that he'd been there, that he was nearer to me than you'd think. It faded quickly, the way dreams do, but it left traces of itself all over my morning, brief pictures of him that stopped me dead and got my heart pounding, as if he was suddenly there in the room, and I only had to turn my head to see him.

And while I pretended to myself that it wasn't impossible, while I imagined Thurston on his way, leaving home and at the airport, taking a taxi, moving towards me, something else happened. I remembered a time, back when I was little. I'd been trying and trying to find them, and suddenly there they were, these snapshots I'd been storing in my head all along.

Ernest, scooping me from my bed like feathers and carrying me outside into the cold night, into the car.

Ernest, on the driver's side, and the car rocking gently when he shut the door.

My mother's hair, loose like dark water, and the jewels on her pearly fingers glistening.

The sky's dark lavender when I sat up and the car turning down towards the sea, as if the whole world was set out below us.

I remember the tide being out, far away on the smooth grey empty sand. I've been at the beach before dawn enough times with Thurston to know how it feels, like you've slipped through a seam in time, the night poised to tip over into day, but not quite, not yet. The edges of things are blurred and grainy and you can't quite see where one ends and another begins. It's all just atoms.

I remember Ernest leaning against the car, watching the waves; Hannah stepping out of her dress and walking barefoot down the long dark stretch to the sea, her slip flowing and gathering around her like mercury in the coming light.

Him taking my hand and pulling me, squealing and

leaping and gasping, across the acres of damp, sucking sand and into the cold, cold arms of the water.

Your heart stops when you go under like that, a sudden quiet in your ears and chest that fills the air like thunder as you break the surface again to breathe. I was a foundling, swimming with my clothes on. I was a water baby.

The brushed-cotton fabric of my nightdress billowing with caught air then clinging to my legs like a heavy second skin, trying to pull me down. Ahead, Hannah's skin flashing white against the gunmetal water as she swam.

Me and Ernest. Ernest and I. We pretended to be washed up after a shipwreck, staggering out of the water and collapsing on to the sand of a far-flung shore, coughing up deep lungfuls of ocean, clinging to life with our fingertips, until we rolled over and I let him pull me upright so we could run at the waves again.

Afterwards I think we must have built a fire. Brushwood and flotsam dragged into a pile on the sand, parched rope and a curl-leafed book, sun-bleached branches from the straggle of trees above the dunes. Ernest showed me how to get the dry grass and the paper and twigs going, how to blow on the flames to make them stronger.

They pulled at me like a magnet. To stare at anything else seemed impossible, seemed plain wrong.

I couldn't have looked away if I'd tried.

In the morning, I didn't think I would ever get up. I held on to those images of my father as hard as I could, when he was young and strong and I knew without question that he loved me.

"Time to go," I said out loud into my empty room in his emptied house. "Time to say goodbye."

Outside on the drive, Hannah and Lowell posed like film stars. I saw Ernest's coffin in the back of the hearse and I tried not to think about him lying in there. I did my very best to look at him and smile.

"Come on then," I said, just in case he could hear me. "Let's get this done."

Twenty-five

Before my last bonfire, before it smouldered against the darkening sky, a man introduced himself and blew open my afternoon. I'd seen him at the service. Tall, with grey hair, rich skin and a charcoal-coloured suit, he came up to me in the garden and smiled.

"You must be Iris," he said.

"I am."

"You look just like Margot," he said, and I said that I knew.

He shook my hand. "I'm Alexander Brown."

I looked around to see if Hannah and Lowell were watching but they were nowhere.

"Did Ernest mention me?"

"I've never heard of you," I said. "I don't think so."

Mr Brown smiled and said, "Good. That's very good."

"Were you friends?" I asked.

"Colleagues. For over thirty years."

"That's nice."

"I'm very sorry for your loss," he said, with his hand on my shoulder, and I thanked him, "Your loss too, I guess."

He asked me to come with him. He said, "There's someone here I think you'd like to meet."

I felt kind of rooted to the spot. I suppose I thought Ernest might still be here somewhere, watching me. What if he was right beside me and I moved away? I didn't want him to feel abandoned.

"What? Now?"

"I think you'll want to. I don't think you'll want to wait."

Alexander Brown slipped a scrap of paper into my hand, and when I looked down it was there in my palm, a drawing of an eye, the round black pupil, the white outline, the bright swirl of colour.

"Thurston?" I said, and I couldn't get the air out of my chest.

He nodded.

"Where is he?" I said. "Is he here?"

Alexander Brown nodded. "He's inside the house."

"Are you kidding me?" I said, and I heard my own voice rising. "Do you mean it? Where? Let me see him. Can I see him right now?"

"Try to stay calm," he said, with his hand over mine. "It's important that we don't attract attention at this stage."

"What stage?"

I sat down hard on a window ledge. All of a sudden, my legs wouldn't hold me any more. I looked up. Birds lined the rooftops of Ernest's house, looking down. They flew up like thrown papers at the first hint of something amiss, at the pop of a champagne cork, at the lick of a lit flame. Thurston told me that birds see everything much faster than us, at so many more frames per second, like a film in fast-forward. That's why they can see danger coming early and why they leave the ground so quick. He said that even if you put the giddiest, most breakneck, edge-of-your-seat action movie on for a bird to enjoy, it would feel like it was watching geriatrics moving underwater. At the time, it made me think of the fire I lit on the pigeon-thick roof of the old Parkway cinema, standing up in the beat and fluster of panicked wings and watching it burn. Now I thought about all the things going on around me that I hadn't been quick enough to see.

"Breathe," Alexander Brown told me, and we did. I sat there and copied his breathing, because I'd forgotten how to do it right on my own.

"How did he get here?" I said.

"Your father."

I smiled. My face broke open and light poured out. That's how it felt.

"Ernest did it? Ernest arranged this?"

"Of course he did."

"How did he find Thurston? How the hell did he do that?"

"He sent the same people who never managed to find you. He made him an offer."

"What offer?"

"One favour for another. Would you like to see him? Are you calm? Shall we go?"

I took another look at the garden, at Hannah and Lowell lording it over the silver service and the smarter sets of guests. There was a cloud over the sun, soft grey and edged with brilliant light. I followed Alexander Brown into the relative dark of the house, where Thurston was waiting.

"He has some important information for you," he said.

"What sort of information?"

"Life-changing. Eye-opening. From Ernest."

"Wait. They spoke?"

"Yes."

"Ernest and Thurston have spoken to each other?"

He blinked very slowly. He said, "It is vital that you compose yourself."

I laughed, following him through the reception rooms and out into the back kitchen.

"You'll need to listen," he said.

I didn't answer him. I couldn't.

Across the room, on the other side of a river of wait staff and canapés and empty bottles, was my best and only friend in the world, tall, dark, skinny, pale, with his arms out ready to catch me, and smiling.

I waded in.

Twenty-six

We found a place to be, just Thurston and me. I held on to his hand and we walked out of the house and away from the funeral party.

"I can't believe he found you," I told him, and Thurston said, "I think that man would have done anything for you."

"So many times," I said, "I thought about how you two would have liked each other, and wished that you could have heard his voice."

"And I did," he said.

"What did he talk to you about?"

We'd got to the place in the woods I'd swept clean, the night of my fire. Thurston stopped walking. "We have to sit down for this. You have to be quiet and try not to interrupt so I can remember it right. You have to do your best just to listen."

"OK," I said. "So what did Ernest tell you?"

"He told me his secrets," Thurston said. "He told me so that I could tell you."

It was because of Margot that Ernest came into his line of work. She was broke and struggling, cut off without a penny, and Ernest said he'd have done anything to help her.

He painted something.

He copied it from the original, which hung in his mum's dressing room. Ernest measured the dimensions, and he got the whites just right. He used old paints. He'd unearthed a box of them in a cupboard somewhere, from his grandfather's time, possibly. He knew enough even then to know that old materials are the lifeblood of a good forger.

Oil on canvas board, eight inches by sixteen, a Charles Courtney Curran painting of the Grand Palais des Beaux Arts in Paris, 1900. Ernest took it to Margot in London. He went on the train on his own. Margot loved it. She thought it was the original, stolen from home.

Ernest told her to sell it. He didn't tell her it was a fake.

And then she phoned him, three weeks later.

"I thought you'd like to know, little brother. That little Curran you stole fetched over ten thousand pounds at auction. Look out for the postman. I'm sending you your cut."

"I didn't steal it," Ernest said. "I painted it."

Margot went quiet. She never went quiet. He thought she was angry with him.

"I'm sorry. I should've told you."

He could hear the grin in her voice before she spoke. "You little genius."

"You don't mind?"

Margot laughed. "Mind?" she said. "God no. I'd never be such a snob. Art's art and all that. Even Michelangelo started out as a forger."

I knew that. When Michelangelo was a struggling artist, he tried to pass off one of his own marble sculptures as an ancient Roman statue, so he could get a better price. With the help of a dealer, he damaged and buried it, so someone would 'discover' it and trick the market.

"Let's do it again," Margot said.

"Do you think we ought to?"

Margot breathed into the phone. "No, but if it's good enough for Michelangelo," she said, "it really should be good enough for us."

That same week she found a willing art historian, a dealer and an expert in his field, and persuaded him to work with Ernest. She met him at a cocktail party. His name was Alexander Brown.

Those are the people with power in the art market, apparently, the experts and dealers. With one dip of the head or tilt of the chin they can make or break a fake painting. Thurston said that Mr Brown was a very useful friend to have. Margot sorted out an introduction. She was going to Mozambique at the end of the month.

"If you want this opportunity," she told Ernest, "you'd better bloody well seize it."

So he did what Margot would have done. He jumped in.

The trick, apparently, wasn't to copy a famous painter, but to become him, the way a method actor inhabits his role. Ernest never copied existing paintings stroke for stroke, not to sell. Instead, he invented other versions of them – abandoned attempts, lost prints, early sketches. He imagined gaps between works.

"Why are there forty-four documented Dali works for the year 1932 and only twenty-eight for 1931?" Thurston asked me. "What did Magritte paint in 1961, after *The Memoirs of a Saint* in 1960 and before *The Great Table* in 1962?"

Art documents itself, and all a good forger had to look

out for was the space between things, the blank days in the diary where you could slip a print, a lithograph, or an undiscovered early work.

"Sold," Thurston told me. "Sold, sold, sold."

To begin with, Ernest said he did pencil drawings in the style of Augustus John and Piranesi and Poussin. Alexander Brown gave him pieces of rare antique paper and he copied on to them, working from catalogues, not originals. But later, he sat in galleries for hours, visiting and revisiting the same works over a period of time, until he understood how they were painted, until he thought he knew just what the artist had seen and felt. The canvases hypnotised him into seeing where they started and how they were begun.

"And by the way, I was right," Thurston told me. "There were artists he wouldn't copy however many times Alexander Brown asked, however much money he might be offered for one."

"Rothko," Thurston said. "According to Ernest, you can't fake a Rothko, and you can't fake an Yves Klein. You'd think they'd be easy, he told me, nothing to it, but they've got the artist all over them. They're the hardest of all."

Ernest concentrated as much as anything on how a

painting or drawing could make him feel. He memorised the first word that came into his head when he looked at the original, so that he could communicate the exact same thing in his copy. Technical accuracy and trails of documents was one thing. That split second, that decisive blink of an eye, was another.

He and Alexander Brown met only once, with Margot, before she went to Mozambique. But they worked together for more than thirty years. Alexander faked records and documents to match most of Ernest's own paintings, and allowed unsuspecting researchers and academics to find them and declare them genuine. Together, they put hundreds of forgeries on the walls of international galleries and private collectors. They exploited the art world's obsession with authenticity to their advantage. The forgeries sold for six and seven figure sums, money Ernest spent on buying genuine paintings, things his mother would have loved, investments. The money he earned by cheating he ploughed straight back in. Maybe it made him feel less guilty, less of a thief.

"Ernest?" I said, when Thurston had finished. "My Ernest? A forger? Why didn't he tell me?"

Thurston was still holding my hand. He hadn't let go of me the whole time he was speaking.

"He said he had to take it to the grave."

My father's fakes were bragged about and shown off and kept under special conditions befitting priceless works by world-famous artists. But nobody had ever heard of Ernest Toby Jones because he never once got caught.

"You know the thing they say about forgeries," Thurston told me. "The good ones are still hanging on the walls."

Twenty-seven

We sat back to back in the woods, looking up at the tops of trees, dark against the sky. I didn't want to move. Thurston looked at his watch. "We have to get back to the house. It's nearly time."

"Time for what?"

He smiled and stood up. "We saved the best till last."

"What best? What now?"

"You'll see."

There was no point asking him what was going on. The day had blown out of my hands like so much ash, like so much powdered paint, and all I could do was wait and see where it landed.

"I do have a fire to light," I said. "I wanted to burn one for him."

He pulled me to my feet. "I'll help with the fire if you like. But let's finish this first."

We walked along the empty road, on the grass verge.

Thurston said, "So there's one more thing. There's something else you need to know. About a letter."

"What letter?"

"A letter that was sent here, and opened and read."

He said I wasn't supposed to see it. He said the letter came through the door as planned while Hannah was still here. It was addressed to Ernest, from Christie's in New York and it was marked URGENT. She took it and read it, and after that, she tore it into tiny pieces and burned it.

"I remember that," I said, that sweet-sharp smell of paper, just burnt, on the stairs, and wondering for a minute who had done it. I remember being worried it was me.

"Why did she do it?" I asked him. "What did it say?"

Thurston smiled and held tightly to my hand. "Just wait."

Back at the house, Alexander Brown was talking to Hannah on the lawn. At Thurston's signal, he came inside to meet us.

He said, "Did your father ever say anything to you about a painting called *Fire Colour One*?"

"He mentioned it, that it meant something. Nothing more than that."

Alexander Brown smiled. "It's yours, a new acquisition."

"Wait," I said. "Ernest owned *Fire Colour One*?"

"Your friend Thurston here manned the telephone at Christie's for Ernest the week before he died."

"You did?" I said, and Thurston nodded.

"He flew me to New York before he flew me here."

Alexander Brown said, "That was the favour I mentioned. Thurston did well. He placed the winning bid. Do you want to know for how much?"

"Not really," I said. "I don't think I do."

"In excess of forty million dollars, Iris," he said. "Ernest's entire worth."

"Forty million dollars?"

"It's yours."

I felt sick. The earth had tilted wildly on its axis and nobody was noticing it but me. That was Forbes List, unforgivable, impossible rich, just like Thurston and I had talked about. I think I reached for his hand. I think without it I might have spun away.

"Can I just keep it?" I said. "The painting, I mean?"

"You can do whatever you want with it," Mr Brown said. "It belongs to you."

"But it doesn't make sense," I told them. "Why the hell would Hannah want me to have it? She told Ernest to let me have the new one. I heard her. Why would she say that if it was worth so much money?"

"Because of this."

He handed me a copy of the letter, the one Hannah had destroyed after reading.

"Read it out loud," he said. "I like the tone of it. Read it to me."

"*We are very sorry to inform you,*" I read, "*that in the light of new documentation... the authenticity of the work entitled FIRE COLOUR ONE... can no longer be confirmed. If you have any concerns or queries... please do not hesitate to contact us. Yours...*"

"It's a fake?" I said. "But you can't fake an Yves Klein. Everyone says it can't be done."

I waited for them both to stop smiling.

"You can't fake an Yves Klein," Alexander Brown said. "You're right. They're too notorious, too well documented. But you can fake a letter. Or I can, anyway."

Hannah intercepted the letter and gave her blessing to my inheritance. In fact it was her suggestion.

Thurston said, "Ernest gave your mother exactly what she asked for. She has no one to blame but herself."

I looked for where she was standing in the garden, a

cluster of people around her, a good tall drink in her hand. She held herself like a coiled spring, triumph leaking through the gaps in her attempt at a sombre surface.

"So we both win," I said.

"Not quite," said Thurston.

"Let's get them in," Alexander Brown said, and I didn't know what he meant.

"What's happening?"

"A moment," Thurston said. "The best one I could think of."

"Where? Here? Now?"

He nodded. "Alexander has persuaded your mother that everyone should have a tour of the paintings, before they get taken down and sold."

Before I could say anything, he put a heavy torch in my hand and said, "There's going to be a power cut. It's going to get very dark in those rooms with the curtains drawn. You'll need this."

The guests were already coming in. The room was filling up. Alexander Brown stayed with me and Thurston slipped behind a pillar as Hannah pushed her way through to the front.

"This," she said, spreading her arms wide, "is the Italian room."

When Ernest died, before he was even cold, my mother arranged for a crew from London to come and pack up the paintings, wrap each canvas carefully and separately in crates for collection, as soon as he was in the ground. She made appointments with auction houses and private dealers. She was all business and forward motion. She did all that before she even asked me if I was OK. She was looking forward to record-breaking sales, to a bidding war. She was counting her chickens again. She and Lowell must have thought of nothing else.

She stood there, talking about the paintings, counting on her fingers the famous names that graced the walls. Hers now, you could see it written all over her face. All hers.

Alexander Brown shifted a little beside me. He cleared his throat.

"How could he have spent his entire fortune on one painting?" I asked him. "How could he have paid for it, with all these priceless canvasses still on the walls?"

When he said it the first time, I didn't think I'd heard him right. I asked him to say it again, so he did. He said it very quietly, so that nobody else would hear.

"None of the paintings in this house are real."

And as he said it, the lights went out, and the place went black.

"Oh God," Hannah said. "What's happened?"

Not the Vermeer in Ernest's bedroom, Alexander Brown whispered. Not the Miros and Picassos and Modiglianis. Not the Renoir or the Degas or the Van Gogh or the little Gauguins.

"They are all fakes," he said. "Copies of the real thing painted by Ernest in the years since you went missing."

It took my father twelve years to copy his collection. He sold the real works to private collectors on the contractual understanding that they didn't exhibit until a year after his death.

He played the long con.

They were brilliant forgeries. They looked the same on the surface, to the naked eye. They might even have fooled the experts, but underneath they were all worthless.

"Iris has a torch," Thurston said, from somewhere at the back of the room and the crowd parted to let me make my way to the front.

Hannah took it out of my hand. She grabbed it and switched it on, an unexpected warm blue light that made our teeth and the whites of our eyes glow like bulbs.

"What is this, Iris?" she said, and she shone it at the wall.

Ernest had laid traps and my mother stumbled right

into them. There was something beneath the surface of every painting, written in zinc white, so it would show up under ultra-violet and stop my mother and Lowell dead in their tracks. Their world was about to end, and Thurston had made sure they had an audience. Better than my fire, better than any revenge I could ever have thought of, more than twelve years in the making, a message from Ernest for them and one for me too. Hannah checked every one, running from room to room by the end of it, followed by a stream of witnesses, hysterical, apocalyptic, catastrophic.

The same word on each of the forty-seven canvasses that filled the house. Bigger and bigger each time until it took up the whole space, waiting patiently, screaming out beneath layers of paint.

IRIS.

Acknowledgments

Thanks Thanks Thanks to Veronique Baxter and Bob Ricard, Rachel Denwood, Alex, Molly and Ella.

'Finding Violet Park traces a journey
we all have to make.'
Guardian

FINDING VIOLET PARK

Jenny Valentine

There were reasons why Violet Park should have meant
nothing to me. She was old. She was dead. She was in a
box on a shelf. But I met her one night, by accident, in
the middle of the night and she changed everything.

When sixteen-year-old Lucas Swain rescues
Violet Park's ashes from a mini-cab office, he
sets out to discover who she was, and finally
faces up to the question of his missing father…

ONE

The mini cab office was up a cobbled mews with little flat houses either side. That's where I first met Violet Park, what was left of her. There was a healing centre next door – a pretty smart name for a place with a battered brown door and no proper door handle and stuck on wooden numbers in the shape of clowns. The 3 of number 13 was the letter w stuck on sideways and I thought it was kind of sad and I liked it at the same time.

I never normally take cabs but it was five o'clock in the morning and I was too tired to walk anywhere and I'd just found a tenner in my coat pocket. I went in for a lift home and strolled right into the weirdest encounter of my life.

It turns out the ten pounds wasn't mine at all. My sister Mercy had borrowed my coat the night before – without asking – even though boys' clothes don't suit her and it was at least two sizes too big. She was livid with me about the money. I said maybe she should consider it rent and wouldn't the world be a better place if people stopped taking things that didn't belong to them?

It's funny when you start thinking about pivotal moments like this in your life, chance happenings that end up meaning everything. Sometimes, when I'm deciding which route to take to, say, the cinema in Camden, I get this feeling like maybe if I choose the wrong route, bad stuff will happen to me in a place I never had to go if only I'd chosen wisely. This sort of thinking can make decisions really really difficult because I'm always wondering what happens to all the choices we decide not to make. Like Mum says, as soon as she married Dad she realised she'd done the wrong thing and as she was walking back down the aisle, she could practically see her single self through the arch of the church door, out in the sunlight, dancing around without a care in the world, and she could have spat. I like to picture Mum, dressed like a meringue with big sticky hair, hanging on to Dad's arm and thinking about gobbing on the church carpet. It always makes me smile.

Whatever, Mercy decided to borrow my coat and she forgot to decide to remove the money and I decided to spend the whole night with my friend Ed in his posh mum's house (Miss Denmark 1979 with elocution lessons) and then I made the choice to take a cab.

It was dark in the Mews, blue-black with a sheen of orange from the street lamps on the high street, almost dawn and sort of timeless. My shoes made such a ringing noise on the cobbles I started to imagine I was back in time, in some Victorian red light district. When I stepped into the minicab office it was modern and pretty ugly. One of the three strip lights on the ceiling was blinking on and off, but the other two were working perfectly and their over-brightness hurt my eyes and made everyone look sort of grey and pouchy and ill. There were no other punters, just bored sleepy drivers, waiting for the next fare, chain smoking or reading three-day-old papers. There was a framed map of Cyprus on one wall and one of those gas fires that they reckon are portable with a great big bottle you have to fit in the back. We had one like that in the hostel when we went on a school journey to the Brecon Beacons last year. Those things are not portable.

The controller was in this little booth up a few stairs with a window looking down on the rest of them and you could tell he was the boss of the place as well. He had a cigar in his mouth and he was talking and the smoke was going in his eyes so he had to squint, and the cigar was bouncing up and down as he talked and you could see he thought he was Tony Soprano or someone.

Everybody looked straight at me when I walked in because I was the something happening in their boring night shift and suddenly I felt very light headed and my insides were going hot and cold, hot and cold. I'm pretty tall for my age but them all staring up at me from their chairs made me feel like some kind of weird giant. The only person not staring at me was Tony Soprano so I kind of focused on him and I smiled so they'd all see I was friendly and hadn't come in for trouble. He was chomping on that cigar, working it around with his teeth and puffing away on it so hard his little booth was filling up with cigar smoke. I thought that if I stood there long enough he might disappear from view like an accidental magic trick. The smoke forced its way through the cracks and joins of his mezzanine control tower and it was making me queasy so I searched around, still smiling, for something else to look at.

That's when I first saw Violet. I say "Violet" but that's stretching it because I didn't even know her name then and what I actually saw was an urn with her inside it.

The urn was the only thing in that place worth looking at. Maybe it was because I'd been up all night, maybe I needed to latch on to something in there to stop myself from passing out, I don't know, I found an urn. Halfway up a wood panelled wall, log cabin style, there was a shelf with some magazines on and a cup and saucer, the sort you find in church halls and hospitals. Next to them was this urn that at the time I didn't realise was an urn, just some kind of trophy or full of biscuits or something. It was wooden, grainy and with a rich gloss that caught the light and threw it back at me. I was staring at it, trying to figure out what it was exactly. I didn't notice that anyone was talking to me until I got the smell of cigar really strongly and realised that the fat controller had opened his door because banging on his window hadn't got my attention.

"You haven't come for her, have you?" he asked and I didn't get it but everyone else did because they all started laughing at once.

Then I laughed too because them all laughing was funny and I said, "Who?"

The cigar bobbed down towards his chin with each syllable and he nodded towards the shelf. "The old lady in the box."

I didn't stop laughing, but really I can't remember if I thought it was funny or not. I shook my head and because I didn't know what else to say I said, "No, I need a cab to Queens Crescent please," and a driver called Ali got up and I followed him out to his car. I walked behind him down the mews and out into the wider space of the high street.

I asked Ali what he knew about the dead woman on the shelf. He said she'd been around since before he started working there, which was eighteen months ago. Somebody had left her in a cab and never collected her and if I wanted to know the whole story I should speak to the boss whose name I instantly forgot because he was always Tony Soprano to me.

The sun was coming up and the buildings with the light behind them looked like their own shadows, and I thought, how could anyone end up on a shelf in a cab office for all eternity? I'd heard of Purgatory, the place you get to wait in when Heaven and Hell aren't that sure they want you, but I'd never thought it meant being stuck in a box in Apollo Cars forever. I couldn't get the question out of my head, felt it burrowing down to some dark place in my skull, waiting for later.

Thinking about it now, it's all down to decision making again, you see. My better self didn't get in the cab straight away that morning. My better self strode right back in and rescued Violet from the cigar smoke and the two-way radio and the instant coffee and the conversation of men who should have known better than to talk like that in front of an old lady. And after liberating her from the confines of the cab office, my better self released her from her wooden pot and sprinkled her liberally over the crest and all the four corners of Primrose Hill while the sun came up.

But my real self, the disappointing one, he got in the car with Ali and gave him directions to my house and left her there alone.

My name is Lucas Swain and I was almost sixteen when this began, the night I stayed too late at Ed's house and met Violet in her urn. Some things about me in case you're interested. I have a mum called Nick and a dad called Pete (somewhere) and a big sister called Mercy, the clothes borrower, who I've mentioned. She's about at the peak of a sarcastic phase that's lasted maybe six years already. I also have a little brother called Jed.

Here's something about Jed. On the days I take him to school he always thinks up a funny thing to tell me. We are always at the same place when he tells me this funny thing, the last stretch once we've turned the corner into Princess Road. You can tell when Jed's thought of something early because he can't wait to get there, and on the days he's struggling to come up with it he drags his feet and we end up being late, which neither of us minds. The punch line is my brother's way of saying goodbye.

The other cool thing about Jed is that he's never met our dad and he's not bothered. Dad went missing just before Jed was born so they've never set eyes on each other. Jed doesn't know him at all.

There's a lot of that with Dad, the not knowing. Mum slags him off for abandoning us, and I half listen and nod because it makes her feel better. But I worry that she's not being fair because if he got hit by a bus or trapped in a burning building or dropped out of a plane, how was he supposed to let us know?

I saw a film once about an alien who landed on earth in a human body in a mental hospital. He had all this amazing stuff to teach everyone and he kept telling the doctors who he was and where he was from and what he had to offer in the way of secrets of the universe and stuff, but they just thought he was mad and pumped him full of drugs and he stayed there until he died. Maybe something like that happened to my dad. He wants more than anything to call us and it's been five years, and wherever he's locked up he's not allowed to phone and he's just waiting for us to find him. This sort of thought, and other variations, occur to me at least once every day.

Like I said, it's the not knowing that's hard.

TWO

Ali dropped me off in his cab and even though everyone was about to get up at home I went straight to bed. Mum walked past my room a couple of times in her pyjamas, giving me her special "You stayed out too late" look, but I pretended not to notice.

I lay there for ages but I couldn't sleep. Jed had Saturday morning telly on too loud. Mum was joining in with something really lame on the radio. Mercy had found my coat on the stairs and was slamming doors and ranting about the money I spent getting home, but it wasn't them keeping me awake. All that's quite normal for a Saturday and I usually sleep right through. Every time I closed my eyes, the urn was there on its crappy shelf, glaring at me, which was unsettling and made me open my eyes again. It was the strangest feeling, being reproached by an urn.

I got out of bed and put my clothes back on and went for a walk on the heath. It was a beautiful day, all vast blue sky and autumn colours and a clean breeze that made me forget I'd had no sleep, but I couldn't relax into it. That part of the heath is covered with enormous crows. They've got massive feet and they walk around staring at their massive feet like they can't believe how big they are. They all look like actors with their hands behind their backs, rehearsing the bit in that play when the king says, "Now is the winter of our discontent..."

I watched them for a while and then I walked up to the top of kite hill and ate an apple. You can see the whole of London from up there pretty much: St Paul's, the Telecom tower, the buildings at Canary Wharf and the docks. There were a few runners on the athletics track just below me and plenty of dog walkers and little kids, but not many old ladies and that set me wondering what all the old people who live in London got up to with their time.

What did the old lady in the cab office do before she did nothing all day in that urn?

Did she get up really, really early in the morning like most old people? Mum says that's their work ethic, the same reason old men wear suits and ties instead of tracksuit bottoms, and old ladies queue up outside the post office half an hour before it even opens and have really clean curtains and stuff. But doesn't getting up that early just mean there are more hours to fill with being old?

Before then I'd never thought what it was actually like to be a pensioner. I'd just weaved in and out of them on the pavement, and smirked with my friends at their funny hair and high-waisted trousers, and the way they make paying for something at a checkout last for ages just to have someone to talk to. One minute the thought never crossed my mind, the next I was really and truly concerned about what it was like to be old and stuck in London, where everyone moved faster than you and even the simplest thing could end up taking all day.

It was her. I know it was. It was my old lady, the dead one in the urn.

I remember sitting there on the hill with kites whipping through the air behind me and the thought occurring to me that she and I might actually be having some kind of conversation. A dead old lady was trying to educate me about the over-sixties from her place on the shelf. It was a good feeling, a hairs-on-the-back-of-your-neck feeling, like when you hear a wicked bit of music, or when you're high and someone you're really into is sitting next to you. I suspected I was making it up but that hardly mattered. I make a lot of things up that are important to me, like being irresistible to girls, or being moody and mysterious like my dad, or what my dad might be up to at any moment, even this one.